The Iron Relic
Origins

Bobby Hundley / James Stevenson

ON THE BOARDS PUBLISHING

On The Boards Publishing

1005 East Las Tunas Blvd, #236

San Gabriel, CA 91776

Editor: FirstEditing.Com

ISBN-10: 0-9863006-2-4

ISBN-13: 978-0-9863006-2-2

Library of Congress Control Number: 2015920165
On The Boards Publishing, San Gabriel, CA

Rv04

Printed in the United States of America.

Visit The Iron Relic Book Series on the World Wide Web at

www.theironrelicbook.com

DEDICATIONS

To all of the men and women who have fought for freedom.
James Stevenson

To my children, Elaine and Brandon, you make my heart complete. To my beautiful, spirited sisters, who have shown me continual kindness and unconditional love, Heather, Corinne, and Amy.
Bobby Hundley

SEPTEMBER 1914

Henry Calhoun was the tall, handsome, and healthy son of Matthew and Catherine Calhoun. Matthew served the community, which respected him as a fair and honest police officer, while Catherine was a modern woman working at the post office as a telegraph operator. Next to their faith, Henry's parents valued education above all else. They had continually emphasized to Henry, throughout his formative years, that the key to advancement in society was education. After Henry completed secondary school, receiving high marks and excelling in Latin, Greek and mathematics, his father had hoped Henry would elect to study for a career in medicine while at University College, Dublin. Instead, Henry chose to receive his tutelage from Professor Eoin MacNeill in their school of history while taking a great interest in rugby and, judging by Henry's muscular features, his time spent playing for the rugby football club had paid off.

Professor MacNeill once described Henry in a student evaluation as "A natural leader, a devout Catholic, well spoken, highly intelligent, and a bit of a prankster. In short, young Mr. Calhoun, has the makings of a charming gentleman with unwavering courage, honor, and principles." Henry looked up to his father, who raised him to believe that Irishmen were the bravest men in the world. And he adored his mother, who raised him to believe the purpose of that bravery was intended for a service to others less fortunate. This day would prove to be the day Henry stepped out on his own and away from the security his parents had provided for him.

Henry's father had achieved the rank of sergeant during the Boer Wars and retired from service in 1902. During his time overseas, he was struck with an illness that rendered him unable to sire further children, leaving Henry his only child. The family moved to Dublin in 1904 when his father took up a position as a constable in The Royal Irish Constabulary, the armed police force of the United Kingdom in Ireland. Matthew Calhoun was a stern man, but he adored Henry. Being a soldier himself, he understood Henry's desire to explore the world and fight for something greater than himself. But in his aging years, Henry's father had become more outspoken on his political views for a united Ireland, and even though he supported the Great War, he would have preferred for his son to stay home and make use of his education. However, Henry put it simply to his father: he was not interested in politics, and God needed brave Irishmen to enact justice in the world. Matthew knew then that his son was his own man and bestowed his blessing on Henry to enlist in a special company that was opening up in his former regiment, the Royal Dublin Fusiliers.

Henry's mother, on the other hand, admired her son's sense of adventure. "The only true way to forge a man of substance is from within the man himself," she would tell Henry. She seemed to understand his sense of restlessness, even if that led her son to follow his pals onto the battlefield. And so Henry swept his mother's beautiful blonde locks from the side of her face and kissed her on the cheek.

Catherine removed a simple necklace from around her neck. "Here. Take this so you'll always have a piece of home," she said as she lifted the necklace over Henry's head and placed it around his neck. A clasped, oval-shaped locket hung from the necklace. Inside the locket was a picture of his parents.

"I'll cherish it and return it home safely to you," Henry promised. He then turned, looked his father directly in the eyes, and shook his hand. In that moment, he was able to see both pride and fear in his father's eyes.

The elder Calhoun embraced his son and spoke into his ear, "For the glory of Ireland."

Henry held his father tightly and replied in kind, "For the glory of Ireland."

Henry then stepped out into the street and gave one final wave and smile to his parents. If he knew this would be the last time he would look into his father's eyes, then perhaps he would never have opted to enlist, but then again, fortunes are made from men of strong nerves and will. Matthew took Catherine in his arms, and the loving couple watched Henry stride off towards the heart of the city.

Henry chose to take the long way to the temporary recruitment station that had been set up for the Irish Rugby Football Volunteers at Lansdowne Road. He wanted to enjoy one last look at some of the more memorable places for him in his hometown. He strode down Patrick Street and then crossed between St. Patrick's Park on his left and St. Patrick's Cathedral on his right. This was the route he had taken frequently with his beloved Deirdre on their chaperoned, afternoon constitutionals during their year-long courtship. As Henry turned down Bride Street, his heart grew uneasy and his mind began to wander towards thoughts of Deirdre. He clenched his jaw, took a deep breath, and tried hard to suppress the feelings he had for the dark-haired, blue-eyed beauty. The past several weeks had been torture for Henry, as if the devil himself had been painting a masterpiece of heartbreak on the young man's soul.

He drifted down Peter Street and over onto Whitefriar Street, where he found himself standing in front of his favorite building in all of Dublin, Whitefriar Street Church. The beautiful, Byzantine interior of the Carmelite church beheld an impressive collection of white arches that rose above apricot-colored pillars towards the yellow, cathedral-like ceiling. A glorious collection of stained-glass windows that seemed to speak directly to the souls of each visitor were the perfect compliment to the shrines that were housed within the church walls, including the shrine that protected the bones of St. Valentine's blessed body. Henry had spent much time of late in reflection within these holy walls, most of it spent before his favorite set of stained-glass windows known as the Rosary Windows, which depicted scenes from the life of Our Lady. The one flaw of this exquisite structure was that the extraordinary interior was cloistered by an equally unimpressive, dull grey exterior. Henry believed that this was perhaps the Lord's way to remind him to never forget to love those who are humble in appearance because inside, their spirit is of great worth and beauty.

On this afternoon, Henry felt more like the way the outside of the building looked than the inside. Several weeks earlier, he came to the steps of the church dressed in his Sunday best with a bouquet of vibrant Irish wildflowers in one hand and his other hand set nervously inside his pant pocket, where his grandmother's ring rested. The ring was a gift from his grandmother to him with the understanding that he would present it one day to his bride to be. Henry had planned to present the ring to Deirdre during their walk and declare to the world his love for the dearest creature to enchant his heart. As the hour drew near for her arrival, beads of sweat encircled his neckline, under arms, and palms until suddenly a high-pitched voice called out to him. Henry turned eagerly, only to find a young lad bearing a rolled-up piece of parchment tied with a strand of twine. The lad worked for Deirdre's family.

"For you, sir," the young boy said as he handed the note over to Henry.

Henry took the note and stood silently as the boy hurried off down the street. Was his beloved ill or had something worse befallen her? He gently removed the twine, opened the parchment, and read the note. After a moment, his hand fell to his side, clutching the note in his palm. His fingers slowly began to squeeze the parchment until his grip was so firm that the ink itself seemed to weep off the parchment and slip through his tightened fist. The note was simple to a fault. She was gone—but gone without sufficient reason, at least one sufficient for Henry to accept: Deirdre simply wrote, "I love another."

In that moment, Henry felt as if his complete understanding of love had died with those three simple words. No longer would he feel the delicate nudge of her forehead upon his shoulder as she gripped her arms around his bicep and held him so close that he could feel her ribs touch his with each excited inhale. During their walks together, he had felt as though she had claimed his heart as hers and hers as his, but now he knew those thoughts were only the fantasies of a silly school boy dreaming of love—a ruse that would drive him to long to feel alive once again, to feel a part of something greater, and to drown out the pain—a ruse that would drive him to war. The rough clopping of horses passing snapped Henry out of his painful daydream of self-pity. He took one last look at the church and continued towards the recruitment station.

Once he reached Lansdowne Road, Henry stood in

line and waited patiently with a number of other individuals, many of them sportsmen he was familiar with from the Rugby Club. These patriotic men had risen to the call put out by the president of the Irish Rugby Football Union and were daily turning out in droves to fill out and sign their attestation papers and head off for military training in the new "D" company that was opened up just for them. After an hour or so, Henry's time had come. Pen in hand, he stared down at the papers.

Henry must have taken quite a long pause because the recruiting officer barked at him, "You illiterate?"

Henry glanced up from the forms, ready to knock the British recruiting officer right between the eyes for uttering such an offensive remark, but then thought better of it. He restrained himself and simply shook his head, "No."

The recruiting officer continued, "Right then, hurry up."

The first question on the form was, "What is your surname?" to which Henry wrote, "Calhoun." The next question was, "What are your Christian names?" to which Henry wrote: "Henry."

It's all downhill from here, Henry thought as he continued to fill out the form. That was, until a single question near the end of the form made him pause. "Are you a British subject?" Henry lifted his pen for a moment and then wrote down his answer: "Yes." Little did Henry know that drastic changes would lie ahead for his country while he fought in a foreign land.

The next part of the form was his oath. The oath was typed in, with a blank section for his name and an area for his signature at the bottom. Henry read the oath to himself quietly, "I, _____, do make oath, that I will be faithful and bear true Allegiance to His Majesty King George the Fifth, His Heirs, and Successors in Person, Crown and Dignity, against all enemies." He stopped reading aloud, continuing silently in his head until he hit the part that said, "So help me God." *So help me God.* A sense of loyalty to his father, to his mother, and to his countrymen came over him. He was Irish and proud. Could he truly make such an oath with God as his witness? Henry raised his pen and filled in the blank with one minor adjustment. Henry, like many of his Irish brothers in arms, purposely misspelled his name. "I, Henri Calhoun, do..." and then signed it, Henri Calhoun (signature of recruit).

Henry joined the rest of the gentlemen of "D" Company, 7th Battalion, Royal Dublin Fusiliers, also known as the 7th Dublins, the Dubs, or the Pals, in

Phoenix Park. There the men were put through rigorous trench warfare training in order to prepare them for the advances in modern warfare, heavy artillery, and high explosives. The congested Phoenix Park served as the first stop in a strenuous nine-month stretch of company training, musketry, elementary drill, platoon, and night operations before the company was inspected by King George V himself.

In spite of the limited months of training, the men of the Dubs displayed tremendous confidence, discipline, and were eager to go and fight. By June 1915, the 7th Battalion was deemed ready for combat. Rumors spread amongst the men that they were destined for France, but then in July they received contradictory orders. They were now headed to the Mediterranean with the final destination unknown. The upper brass intended to ship the 7th Battalion to Gallipoli as part of the Mediterranean Expeditionary Force, whose objective was to take control of the Dardanelles and aid in the capture of the Ottoman capital of Constantinople. The Dardanelles Straights provided a major access point for forces from Europe to go to Russia by connecting the Black Sea to the Mediterranean. Control of this route would give Allied forces a powerful, strategic advantage in the region.

Henry and his fellow Fusiliers were given only several days of notice to prepare for their journey, and they found themselves severely ill-equipped. The months of training had left many men with worn out or incomplete uniforms and badly distressed leather equipment. In addition, the men of the 10th Division, from the regimental officers on down, knew nothing of the actual plan or objectives of this campaign on the Gallipoli Peninsula in order to properly prepare for the geographical challenges of the region, but this did little to dampen their mood. This was the moment the men had been waiting for, and they were overjoyed to finally be on the move.

The officers and NCOs went to work promptly, ensuring all of the men were re-equipped with new belts and accoutrements and had any necessary adjustments made to their khaki uniforms and helmets before they finished packing their kit bags and set sail on the *Alaunia*. Once on board the former ocean liner, Henry and his pals stayed in high spirits throughout the journey, as they made stops in places he had only studied about: Gibraltar, Malta, and now the breathtaking harbor of Alexandria, Egypt.

A pack of men, including Henry, jogged in formation around the deck as the sun rose in the east. Henry took a deep breath in through his nose, allowing a rush of crisp sea air to fill his lungs and energize his soul. He found the daily jogs to not only be therapeutic but also build a strong sense of camaraderie amongst the men. These pals were a tight-knit group that set aside any differences in religion and politics and united as brothers in arms. In their downtime, the men would sing songs, smoke, and play cards on one of the three decks. As he exercised, Henry smiled to himself, blocking out all sounds except the thump of his boots hitting the steel deck of the ship as it sliced through the deep blue Mediterranean Sea. In that moment, he felt that this was a life he was more than well suited for. As the men charged around the stern and headed for the bow of the ship, the west harbor of the Port of Alexandria came into view. Henry's eyes lit up at the sight of the stunning harbor, and he suddenly felt the history and the magnitude of it on him, taking him back in time.

Founded by Alexander the Great, Alexandria had been home to some of the greatest philosophers, scholars, and mathematicians of their age—Eratosthenes, Archimedes, and Euclid—and had served as home to the tragic romance between Cleopatra and Mark Antony, who was rumored to have given Cleopatra a wedding gift of 200,000 books for the legendary library built under Ptolemy I sometime between 306 and 288 BC. The handwritten papyrus scrolls contained within the ancient library and a secondary library in the Temple of Serapis were more valuable than gold and would be priceless in Henry's time. Legend had it that each ship that sailed into Alexandria's harbor was searched and would have any scrolls aboard seized. These scrolls would then be reviewed by one of the library's many scholars. If the scroll was deemed to contain elements of historical, philosophical, or cultural significance, then the book would be copied by hand and returned to its owner.

Henry recalled from his studies at University College that early Christians used the Septuagint, the oldest known Greek translation of the Old Testament, as their standard text. The Septuagint was believed to have been completed by 72 Jewish scholars, who were asked by King Ptolemy to translate the Torah into Greek. Oh, what Henry would give to be able to browse through the stacks of the greatest library the world had ever seen. Unfortunately, that would not be a tourist attraction during his short leave in Alexandria. The Library of Alexandria had been destroyed over the years, and many of these scrolls of knowledge were believed to have been burned and lost forever.

The distant echo of bombing snapped Henry from his daydream and back into the reality of war, as the *Alaunia* dropped anchor. While Henry and the rest of the men prepared to disembark, a series of boats bearing the emblem of the Red Cross on their port side drifted into the busy harbor. Medical orderlies worked relentlessly bandaging the wounded on board. Henry watched as a male orderly, a corporal with a circular Red Cross patch above his insignia, tended to a young soldier, whose face was covered in grease and clay. The young soldier had a bandage around his head and across his torso. The boat was met onshore by a combination of Australian nurses and members of the Royal Army Medical Corps, who were carrying stretchers to load the wounded onto waiting ambulances for transport to the hospitals in Alexandria.

One Australian nurse, wearing a grey dress, white blouse, and apron, quickly approached the corporal and the injured, young soldier. Her face revealed the signs of someone who had committed long hours of tireless service, and her demeanor revealed a desensitized quality that accompanied someone who had continually witnessed the gruesome sights of war. Two men from the RAMC brought a stretcher to her side to load the injured soldier. She reached for the injured soldier before the Red Cross corporal could warn her of the extent of his injuries. As she gently took the young soldier by the hand, the men from the RAMC lifted him onto the stretcher, causing the young soldier's splintered hand to separate completely from his wrist. Henry had never witnessed anything like this in his life. The hand had been held together by putty and bandages. The nurse fell backwards onto the muddy ground with the soldier's hand in hers. She quickly rose to her feet and continued on with her duties aiding the injured soldier. By now, Henry noticed his pals were on either side him, watching in silence as the Red Cross unloaded the wounded.

After a few minutes, the men of the 7th were ordered to disembark and fall into formation once on land. The battalion was surrounded by soldiers from other divisions and other countries who were milling about their makeshift camps. Henry was shocked to find a high number of Egyptian reporters unashamedly photographing the soldiers as they drilled. The reporters were clumped in with fishermen and other locals, who seemed to take a keen interest in watching the battalion's every move. Unbeknownst to the soldiers, many of these locals were making a side income by taking notes and selling that information nightly to German agents, who were hiding in the dark under belly of the city. Or perhaps it was that their Allied commanders knew about this exchange of information but viewed it as the price to do business in Alexandria, so to speak, because even the daily Egyptian newspapers were printing detailed accounts of the movement of the British forces. The 7th would serve as reinforcements to the initial attack, which had suffered disastrous losses. The initial landing in Gallipoli was so bungled that there were even reports that a French general had given an interview to an Egyptian newspaper detailing the Allied tactics for invading the peninsula prior to the invasion. Needless to say, the Turkish forces were well informed and well prepared for the initial attack.

Once on land and in formation, the men of the 7th were marched around Alexandria's harbor and then ordered to resupply at the Army Service Corps store within the city. Henry headed to the store with one of his mates, Private Robert McDonough, a cocky but good-natured fellow from Dublin. Henry knew him from the Rugby Club, and McDonough's crooked nose was a friendly reminder of the good old days on the pitch. After picking up their supplies and a postcard featuring Alexandria's port and famous lighthouse, the two journeyed into the heart of Alexandria's Arabian bazaar.

The city was bustling with life; everyone was shoulder to shoulder as Henry and McDonough passed through the colorful marketplace. There was all manner of people, with some dressed in long, cotton garments dyed an assortment of colors, while others were dressed in the fashions of Europe. Fabric awnings were pitched out from the store fronts, providing much-needed shade from the midday sun. Under one awning, a street performer baffled and amazed the men as he drove nails into different parts of his body with ease. Henry, with his phrase book in hand, did his best to search out a decent café while McDonough haggled with one of the local vendors over the price of a tin of fruit and some sweets. After settling on a price and feeling quite victorious, McDonough took his tin and package of sweets and followed Henry into a nearby café.

The corner café was filled with smoke and bustling with soldiers in uniform. Men in khaki drill tunics, the lighter weight version of the thick woolen service dress tunic, filled the café. McDonough quickly scanned the room for officers and saw none. "No brass hats," McDonough said as he gave Henry a firm pat on the shoulder.

As the two men entered the smoky, shaded room, Henry noticed that nearly every man in the café had traded his bucket hat for a red, felt, truncated-cone hat the locals called a fez. Henry spied a small, empty table toward the back. He headed toward the table, but after a few steps, he stopped in his tracks and hesitated a moment. The table was surrounded by older veteran soldiers and a few local young boys, who were most likely employed by the soldiers to run messages and make small purchases for the soldiers while they relaxed and enjoyed their time away from battle.

"What's the matter?" McDonough asked.

"It's all old sweat back there. I'm not sure they'll want us rookies in their space," Henry replied with a sense of caution.

"Don't be a gimp," McDonough said as he pushed Henry to the table.

Once seated, McDonough placed his tin and package on the worn table. He then reached into his upper left breast pocket and pulled out a small cardboard pack of cigarettes.

"Gasper?" he asked as he offered one to Henry.

"Wild Woodbine?" Henry asked as he took the cigarette and put it between his lips.

"Is there any other?" McDonough replied as he lit a match and held it out for Henry.

"Yes, and some are actually good." Henry coughed as he settled back into his chair.

Sensing this might just be their last opportunity to have a decent meal for quite some time, Henry and McDonough ordered to their hearts content, starting with a couple pints of beer.

Henry raised his beer. "To your health."

"To your health," McDonough replied, clinking his mug against Henry's.

There was something comforting about the beer, something civilized to the whole affair of their dinner. Henry and McDonough no longer felt like soldiers headed for a valley of death but rather like two pals, laughing and enjoying a pint back home in Dublin. They took their time, savoring each bite of their large supper, which consisted of a variety of grilled meats, a type of baguette-like bread called *aysh*, and beans. Once the main course had settled nicely into their stomachs, the men enjoyed another smooth smoke and finished off sweets covered in a honey syrup before rejoining the others back on board the *Alaunia*.

Next up for the men of the 7th Dublin Fusiliers was a quick stop in Mudros Bay, off the Island of Lemnos, and then they were off to Mitylene, where the ship would drop anchor and prepare the men for transport to the front lines on the peninsula. Henry and several of his mates relaxed on deck, enjoying the night air as the *Alaunia* steamed ahead to Mitylene. From the expressions on their faces, one might have mistaken the Dubs' final destination as a rugby pitch rather than a no man's land covered in torn, blistered flesh and shrapnel. But make no mistake, these men were chomping at the bit to fight and even downright cheery about it, often breaking into rousing renditions of "It's a Long Way to Tipperary." Besides a thirst to prove themselves in combat, many of the men relished the thought that the fighting would end the dull, monotony of life aboard the ship. Henry was honored to count himself as one amongst them. He believed their valor and spirit to be second to none. To a man, these pals would lay down their life for the brother beside them, and that knowledge alone kept the moral high.

Corporal Christopher Shannon, a slender banker from Dublin, was playing a Dublin card game, House, with Lance-Corporal Deaglan Connors. Connors was a shorter man in his late twenties with a thick build who had left the coal mines of Connaught in search of work in Dublin before enlisting in the army. The service provided him a quick way to better his economic status. He was a bit nervous about the fight ahead, but while others grumbled about the quality of their food, he continued to remind himself that at least here in the army the meal times were consistent.

"I love Ireland, but I can't wait to see what's on the other side of the hill," said Shannon as he reviewed and sorted his cards.

"You're right about that, Christy. My body hasn't felt this good in my whole life," said Sergeant Samuel Brennan, an even-keeled solicitor from Dublin. He stretched out on deck as he sewed a shamrock patch onto the sleeve of his khaki shirt.

"It's all that clean sea air," Henry suggested as he removed his boots.

"Beats the mines," added Connors. "No fears of a mineshaft crashing down on me head out here."

"No, just shells from a German 77." Private McDonough laughed as he bit into a slice of chilled orange. Juice seeped out of the corners of his mouth. "I can't wait to fight. I'm fed up with all this sitting," he continued, irritated. He cupped his hand and wiped the juice from around his mouth and chin.

Lieutenant Montgomery, a smarmy English officer who could barely grow hair under his arms, was walking by and took a cynical interest in the conversation of the men. He had his Pattern Infantry officer's sword in one hand and a wool cloth in the other, polishing the etched blade as he patrolled the deck. Montgomery stopped in front of the battle-hungry private. "You Irish sure love to fight. Why is that, Private McDonough?"

"Surely you know, Mr. Montgomery?" McDonough

asked rhetorically, turning to his mates with a cocky expression on his face. "No disrespect but every Englishman should know that an Irishman is the best damn fighter there is. And what's better than one Irishman? A whole bloody battalion of Irishmen!"

"For the glory of Ireland!" they all cheered.

"I hope you're all still this motivated once the rains of hell are falling down upon us." Montgomery smiled snootily.

"We look forward to performing a jig in it, Lef-tenant. With Saint Patrick by our side, we'll chase the Turkish snakes into the bay and drown them for you so you don't have to dirty your pretty little sword there," Henry boasted.

"And after, we'll turn their no man's land into a football pitch," McDonough crowed as he hit Henry on the shoulder. "You brought the ball, eh, Brennan?"

"Right you are, McDonough. Want to take bets who will score the first goal?" Brennan replied, taking a pocket notebook and small pencil out from his breast pocket.

The young lieutenant just sneered at the men and continued on his tour of the ship, polishing his sword.

The Irishmen took every polite opportunity they could to show their disdain for the incompetent officer. They considered him a school boy officer commissioned out of gentry who was thoroughly lacking in humor. They obeyed him because of his rank, but that didn't mean they respected him. Fighting an enemy set on killing you was a far cry from chasing a fox on horseback. The men of the 7th Service Battalion took tremendous pride in being part of what was considered the first all-Irish division in British history, the 10th Irish Division. Well over seventy-five percent of the servicemen were Irish. Montgomery represented the ten percent or so of officers who were English. But even though the men criticized Montgomery amongst themselves, their loyalty to the division was without question. He was still part of the 10th Division, and disloyalty was not tolerated amongst this fraternity of brothers. They would never portray Montgomery to an outsider as anything but an ideal officer. Within their ranks, however, the men preferred to rally behind their own. For Henry and his mates, those were Irish officers: Captain James Gallager, a charismatic, former professor from Trinity College and Major Fergus Dempsey, a just man, who never missed an opportunity to speak a pleasant word to each of his men in passing.

As the card game pressed on, McDonough continued to air his frustrations to his pals. "I mean, what are we doing? We've been split off from most of our division and stuck cramped together with no information. They didn't even let us get off the ship in Mudros Bay," he grumbled.

"Calhoun, you have the major's ear," Brennan alluded. "Perhaps you would be able to address things for us?"

"I will see what I can do," Henry replied, simply.

Henry was seated on a wooden chair, directly across a small wooden table from Major Dempsey in the major's cabin. Known for his hospitality, Dempsey offered Henry a strong cup of black tea with a healthy helping of milk. Henry thanked the major, took a sip of the tea, and continued relaying the purpose of his visit.

"The men are hardly complainers, sir. They're just anxious to join the fight. All this time at sea is making them idle. They long to have a break in the monotony of ship life, sir," Henry finished.

Dempsey unclasped his hands and lifted his tea cup. "Any suggestions?"

"I was thinking perhaps a concert party is in order."

"A concert?" Dempsey replied, somewhat surprised by Henry's suggestion.

"Yes, sir. There's quite a number of the men who have a bit of musical talent, including our quartermaster."

The major furrowed his brow as he sipped his tea and pondered the idea for a moment. Then he gently set his tea cup on a white porcelain saucer and said, "I believe that is a splendid idea," before looking up at Henry.

"Thank you, Major."

"I might even consider joining in for a song or two if you manage to put together a glee club."

"I'll see what I'm able to do, sir," Henry said with a smile.

"Calhoun, I do require one item of the men. I need your assurance that you and the rest of the men will commit to organizing the set up and subsequent clean up of the event."

"You have my word."

"Right then. Once we anchor in Mitylene, you and the men will have your concert party."

"Thank you, sir, and thank you for your hospitality. That was a wonderful cup of cha." Henry rose from his chair.

"Corporal? Might I ask you a question of personal nature?"

"Of course, sir."

"Why is it that you turned down the opportunity to receive an officer's commission? I learned that when the men had the chance to vote for two of their peers to receive commissions, you received the most votes out of anyone. Yet you turned down the commission. Why is that?"

"A commission would have separated me from my pals, sir. We are a unit of brothers, and if God has me marked to die on the battlefield, I want it to be in the service of their company. That's more important than an officer's sword to me, sir."

"Ireland is proud to have men like you, Mr. Calhoun."

As the sun rose in the eastern grey-blue sky, Henry kneeled solemnly in prayer. After a few minutes, Father Duffey gestured for the men to rise and proceeded to conclude the morning mass aboard the deck of the *Alaunia* with the following words, "As you men are aware, I regrettably will not be with you as you go into battle."

The morning twilight illuminated the uneasy faces of the young men, for many of whom this would serve as their last mass. The thought of death itself was not as troubling to the men as much as the thought of not having their spiritual leader with them. The upper brass had decided that all of the chaplains were to remain with the field ambulance units to tend to the wounded and dying in the hospital tents. Father Duffey understood the distress this would cause many of the men and continued to offer them words of reassurance.

"If you discover yourselves up against

insurmountable odds on the battlefield, remember God's assurance to Moses when Moses felt discouraged and unable to overcome the might of the pharaoh—not too far from this very spot where we pray today, I might add. Moses said to the Lord, 'Lord, wherefore hast thou so evil entreated this people? Why is it that thou hast sent me?' to which God replied, 'Now shalt thou see what I will do to Pharaoh: for with a strong hand shall he let them go, and with a strong hand shall he drive them out of his land.' Carry these words with you and do not fret or fear because our God Almighty will always be by your side. Let us pray."

The men lowered their heads in prayer as the father held his hands up.

"I pray to you dear Lord: just as you aided Moses in setting free the Israelites from the tyrannical rule in Egypt, please instill these men with your might. I pray that you send your angels to serve as an unbreakable wind at the backs of these courageous men and that the swords of your angels protect them. But should you decide to call any of them home, dear Lord, I humbly ask that you judge their souls with mercy, for their cause is just and their hearts are true. Amen."

The men quietly repeated, "Amen," and blessed themselves.

"Peace be with you, my sons."

"And also with you," the men replied with palms upright.

"This mass has ended. Go in peace to love and serve the Lord."

Father Duffey's words brought about a temporary comfort to the men. But to ensure all of the men felt prepared for what lay ahead, he made himself available for the remainder of the day to hear confession and provide spiritual council. After making confession, the men went about their day with gusto in preparation for the evening's concert. The deck was mopped, chairs were lined up row upon row with a stage set in front, and tables for dealing every card game imaginable were quickly set up, filling any remaining space as the deck of the *Alaunia* was transformed into their own private Monte Carlo.

The quartermaster, Edward Lloyd, a bearded man with hazel eyes, rehearsed a glee club comprised of a dozen or so men, including Major Dempsey, in a rendition of William Linley's anthem, "I Called Upon the Lord." Lloyd had the men sounding quite wonderful, considering they had only just begun singing together several days prior. He was a truly gifted choirmaster who spent the better part of his time on the ship composing anthems to

Bible passages. Lloyd had studied music while at Trinity College and was serving as the organist and choirmaster of Trinity Presbyterian Church prior to the outbreak of the war. Tonight he had a special treat for his pals during the concert, and all of the men were keen for its unveiling. Whispers had travelled across the ship revealing that Lloyd would be premiering an original piece entitled "I Bow Down in Mercy, Praise Thee O Lord."

The men knew Lloyd had started composing the piece during basic training while the company was digging trenches on the backside of a hill near Phoenix Park. The piece was inspired on one notoriously stormy occasion. Lloyd had found himself trapped, kneeling down in thick mud with rain crashing down all around him and flooding the trench he had dug. The pounding of the water caused the trench to partially cave in on him, but instead of falling backwards he managed to spring forward on top of the rolling earth. As Lloyd lay prostrated with his palms down on the sticky ground, he looked up and saw the clouds parting and the sun bursting through the crest of the hill. He told the men that he felt as though he was bowing to God's mercy and that he was able to hear the musical notes being played by the sound of each raindrop that fell upon his back. Lloyd would occasionally hum sections of it while the men played cards but never more than a verse. With the call of war and uncertainty ahead of them, he felt now was an appropriate time, and perhaps the only opportunity he would have, to share the composition that he had arranged from bits of Psalm 18:6 to Psalm 18:21.

After spending time in confession, Henry turned the rest of his attention to helping coordinate the arrival of the soldiers from three other ships, including a French vessel. All in all, he felt the evening was sure to be quite the spectacle, with over five hundred men in attendance. Everyone aboard the *Alaunia* genuinely embraced the spirit of the festivities. The Pals had even printed up a concert program detailing the order of the singers and their song selections, along with a headline credit thanking their commanding officers for allowing them to present the evening's concert.

As night fell, the deck of the *Alaunia* lit up, and Major Dempsey took center stage to serve as the evening's emcee. He quickly greeted the crowd of animated soldiers, who playfully heckled him, before introducing the maestro of the evening, Edward Lloyd. Lloyd elegantly took his position as music director before the glee club. With a graceful lift of his hand, the men in the audience fell silent, and the concert took flight as the glee club sang the much-anticipated piece, "I Bow Down in Mercy, Praise Thee O Lord" in a beautiful four-part harmony:

In my distress, In my distress,
I called upon the Lord, I called upon the Lord,
And cried unto my God, Unto my God,
He heard my voice, and my cry,
And my cry came before him.

And so he rode upon a cherub, and did fly:
yea, he did fly upon the wings of the wind.

He sent from above and he took me,
He drew me out of many waters.

And he rode upon a cherub, and did fly:
yea, he did fly upon the wings of the wind.

For in my distress, In my distress,
I called upon the Lord, I called upon the Lord,
And cried unto my God,
He heard my voice, and my cry,
And my cry, came before him.

And he rode upon a cherub, and did fly:
yea, he did fly upon the wings of the wind.

He delivered me from my strong enemy,
And from them which hated me.

For they were too strong for me,
But the Lord was my stay.

The LORD rewarded me, According to my
righteousness;

The LORD rewarded me, According to the cleanness
of my hands,

He recompensed me.

For I have kept the ways of the LORD,
And have not wickedly departed from my God.

So the LORD rewarded me, According to my
righteousness;

The LORD rewarded me, According to the cleanness
of my hands,

He recompensed me with everlasting life.

And the Lord was my stay.

And the Lord was my stay.

And the Lord was my stay.

And the Lord was my stay.

As the last note gave way to silence, Lloyd turned to face the silent soldiers. Several men had their hands clasped as if in prayer, others held their rosaries tight, some just smiled, and others were stone-faced.

Henry sat awestruck, truly touched by the composition, and struggled to hold back the emotion from seeping into his eyes. Next to him, McDonough rose to his feet and gave a hearty applause. This triggered the other men beside him, and soon the entire audience was honoring Lloyd's work with roaring applause. Lloyd bowed politely and moved on to the next musical selection.

As the concert continued, Henry was pleased to find his friends enjoying the event, and he decided to quietly retreat to a more secluded area on the other side of the deck to finish writing a postcard home.

Henry glanced up from his postcard as a burst of fire from exploding artillery shells lit up the distant night sky against the orchestral sounds of the concert aboard the *Alaunia*. The spectacle seemed quite operatic and peaceful to Henry as he reviewed his postcard to ensure it would pass the military censor. He read the letter silently to himself:

We arrived in Mitylene a week ago. Everyone is jolly, having the time of their lives. The major helped arrange a concert for us and a few other outfits aboard the ship. The music is a wonderful distraction. I suppose we will see combat soon. Many men are eager to start fighting. A mate of mine, McDonough, said he was feeling the nervous excitement one might feel before a championship match. I just laughed. I must admit though I am starting to feel idle aboard this boat and am looking forward to the landing ahead. It will be a nice reprieve to stretch our legs and run off some of these Turks. I have seen some magnificent sites. The port of Alexandria truly is the pearl of the Mediterranean. This postcard does not do justice to its splendor, but I hope it will suffice. Know that I am well and love you both dearly.

Your son,

Corporal Henry Calhoun

1st of August, 1915

After enjoying the concert, McDonough sat at a table playing gin rummy and resorted back to his usual grumbling about failing to see action. "The war is going to be a year old in several days, and we have yet to fire a shot in action."

A thin, worn, and weary French soldier who had just returned from action in Gallipoli attempted to give McDonough a few words of advice. "The thirst is worse than any Turkish bullet. The land is a waterless, sunbaked hell only fit for flies. And you'll get those too. Swarms of flies in your eyes, mouth, itching incessantly until your skin is raw and infected, and just when a breeze comes along to rid you of the flies it turns into a dust storm that will make your eyes sting so bad you'll want to pluck them out like Oedipus."

"I take it you've never been to Church Street in Dublin. The rats there are as big as cats. But the rats are the least of your worries. On Church Street, if a building doesn't fall down on you, a manky mentaller with a brutal dose of tuberculosis will try to eat you."

Henry stood at the handrail on the upper deck of the *Alaunia* and stared out across the Mediterranean as the revelry continued on the deck behind him. He began to think back on the past year: the voyage of the *Alaunia* to the training in Phoenix Park to the moment he kissed his mother farewell. His thoughts travelled all the way back and fell on the face of his once beloved Deirdre. The heartsickness he once felt for her had quelled itself with time. But she still held a small, broken corner of his heart. He wondered what had become of her and what might have become of them had she shown up that fateful afternoon. And just like that, the pain of "I love another" kicked him in the gut. At that moment, Henry felt a firm pat on the back. Henry turned to find Major Dempsey by his side.

"Evening Major," Henry said with a nod.

"Congratulations, Corporal. The evening has been quite a success," the major said as he grasped the handrail and looked off in the distance.

"Thank you, sir."

Rockets burst off in the distance, separating the skyline from the glassy ocean surface.

"It is one hell of a sight."

"Sir?"

"The pangs of war." The major replied pensively. "How can a person expect to resolve anything in a Christian manner when they've passed their lives killing?"

"William Shakespeare."

"Tonight brought about a little piece of civilization during a very uncivilized time. It was a great gift to the men." The major patted him once more on the shoulder and continued on a leisurely walk around the ship.

The major's words gave Henry a sense of pride. He looked back out across the sparkling ocean and saw a majestic school of porpoise gliding through the water. *Now is not a time to sulk,* he thought to himself. He drummed the handrail lightly with his fingers and then looked back over his shoulder at his friends playing cards. With one last tap of the rail, he walked off to join his friends at the card table.

On the 6th of August, 1915, the officers of *Alaunia* attended an officers' briefing in the colonel's quarters prior to boarding the men of the 7th onto the armed steamer *HMS Fauvette* destined for Suvla Bay, Gallipoli. The briefing was presided over by their commanding officer, Colonel M. H. Barrington. Barrington was a highly decorated officer who had served in South Africa, Egypt, and India. He was fearless, gallant, and above all else, he was an Irishman with no politics who preferred the company of soldiers to politicians. Shortly after the war broke out, the forty-seven-year-old officer reenlisted to help oversee the new regiment and join the fight for liberty.

Barrington was tasked with leading the men of the 7th in a joint landing on Suvla Bay, involving thousands of soldiers from other divisions. After attending a meeting of the top brass, the colonel found himself highly concerned regarding the overall strategy of the assault. Never a man to mince words, he spoke clearly and directly in expressing his professional opinion to the lieutenant-general tasked with coordinating the attack, General Haultford, who the colonel viewed as a leader in name only. His opinion of Haultford was further justified after the apathetic general completely disregarded the colonel's suggested strategy for the attack. Nonetheless, the colonel had to swallow his pride and relay the general's own half-witted plan to his officers. The officers in attendance were Major Dempsey, Captain Gallager, and junior officers Lieutenant Montgomery and Lieutenant Murray.

"Sir, we learned that the missing artillery pieces were mistakenly shipped to France," quivered Montgomery. "And the Raedeker guide I received that was supposed to detail Turkey, upon further inspection turned out to be a guidebook to the Rhine Valley. In Germany. Sir."

"I am aware of where the Rhine Valley is located, Mr. Montgomery," said a disgusted Barrington. "The men will make due with the munitions we have. Major Dempsey?"

"Suvla Bay is approximately six miles north of Anzac Cove," Dempsey said as he unfolded a hand-drawn map of the coastline that marked the bay and several key hills.

Pointing at the map, he continued, "We have a partial chart, hand-drawn from one of the soldiers we met in Mitylene. We can use that and follow the coastline. We should arrive before dawn."

"Thank you, gentlemen. That is all." Barrington dismissed the officers, leaving him alone with Dempsey. The colonel removed a cigarette from his pocket and lit it. He then turned and offered a smoke to the major. "Cigarette?"

"No thank you, sir." Dempsey said. "Permission to speak freely, sir?"

"Permission granted," Barrington replied, exhaling a long cloud of smoke.

"We are without legitimate maps...low on artillery. What are we expected to attack the Turks with sir, rocks?"

"We have our orders, Major Dempsey," chided the colonel.

"Respectfully sir. What are our orders?"

The colonel removed the cigarette from his mouth and stared out of the window of his cabin. The sky exploded with orange fire in the distance. "To win the war."

"Yes, sir." The major did an about face and stepped toward the cabin's exit.

"Major?"

"Yes, sir."

Barrington adjusted his body towards the major. His eyes had taken on the look of a man who was not willing to send his men to battle on a wing and a prayer. "General Haultford expects Suvla Bay to be weakly guarded. I fear we may find ourselves without definitive orders from the general. When we land, instruct the officers to find cover for the men. I will finalize a strategy for our men once we have had a chance to assess the enemy for ourselves."

"Thank you, sir. I'll prepare the men to board the transport vessels," Dempsey said with a sharp nod of his head.

The men of the 7th were shipped, along with the 6th Battalion, to several double-mast, armed boarding steamers. Henry, along with Connors, Brennan, McDonough, and Shannon, were placed aboard the *HMS Fauvette*. The steamer shoved off with its course set for Suvla Bay, just North of Anzac Cove, where the Australian and New Zealand forces were located and had suffered tremendous losses. The men were packed in tightly, so Henry found the first empty area on the ship he could and set himself down to try and catch a couple hours of shut eye.

A few hours passed, and the pounding of heavy artillery startled Henry awake. He rose to his feet on the deck to see bursts of cannon fire coming from Turkish artillery along the hilltops just inland from the invisible coastline of Anzac Cove. He felt his feet quiver beneath him as the bursting shells caused the entire bay to shutter. A searchlight beam sliced the night sky, hoping to reveal Allied forces. Then as soon as it began, the shelling ceased and the steamer continued up the coast towards Suvla Bay.

The sun didn't dare wake up as the steamer sailed into Suvla Bay. Henry found the lack of Turkish rifle fire and artillery to be surprising and a bit disconcerting. On deck, he noticed that several of the officers seemed confused regarding the landing. Henry overheard Captain Gallager state to Lieutenant Murray that one of the transport steamers had missed the bay completely, continuing to another part of the peninsula. The steamer Henry was aboard dropped anchor. The men quickly began to get their equipment ready for disembarkation but then soon found themselves caught in a waiting game.

The sun rose and the temperature started to skyrocket as the hours passed. Finally, by the time the lighters had floated up alongside the steamers for the parched soldiers to disembark, the minimal Turkish troops defending the coast had already begun gathering reinforcements in the hills behind Suvla Bay. Any advantage the men had was disappearing by the hour. The Dubs boarded the lighters wearing thin, sand-colored khakis with their trousers tucked deep into their putties. Their packs were weighty, filled with a heavy coat, blankets, rations, and over 200 rounds of ammunition. These heavy packs had proved a disadvantage to the first wave of Allied troops who landed months earlier in Anzac Cove. Those troops had been met with a deadly stream of machine gun and cannon fire the moment their beetles approached the beach. The majority of those brave men died before even making it to land. Many were shredded from the blanket of bullets that seemed to cloak the shoreline in death. Others desperately jumped overboard in a frantic attempt to swim for shore only to find themselves sinking to the bottom of the cove and drowning under the weight of their packs in the blood-stained water.

The ultimate goal of the landing at Suvla Bay was to secure a northern base on this beach in order to support the troops who were locked in a deadly stalemate with Turkish defenses down in Anzac Cove. The generals in charge of the Suvla Bay operation bickered back and forth about how to accomplish that. Colonel Barrington's recommendation to General Haultford prior to the assault was that if the ground was lightly held by the Turks, then his men should advance inland and seize control of the hills surrounding the bay. General Haultford instead chose to order the men to reach the beach, rest up, and wait for any further action until all forces had been consolidated. This reply was one of a man who clearly failed to realize the importance of a swift and aggressive offensive in winning battles. But for now, the colonel and his officers focused on getting their men to the beach.

Henry double-checked his kit bag for his bayonet and entrenching tool. Then Henry took the water bottle he had emptied from thirst and clipped it to his belt next to a homemade leather sheath that held his father's old field knife. Henry removed a rosary from his pocket, kissed it, returned it to his pant pocket, and boarded the flimsy lighter.

The full scope of the chaotic landing came into view as the lighters rowed towards the beach. Some of the transport steamers had tried to disembark their men throughout the night under the cover of darkness, but in the confusion, the regiments became intermingled and separated. A couple of the lighters had smashed into reefs and dangerously plunged their occupants into neck-deep waters with the 60 pound kits strapped on their backs. Henry and his mates searched the clay cliffs and shrub-covered hillsides inland for enemy snipers and artillery as shots rained down at the troops on the beach. The enemy fire was sporadic, with the occasional artillery shell bursting in the cove and sending a number of stunned fish to the surface.

The world seemed to change before Henry's very eyes. Henry took a deep breath, heeding his father's advice before he left home for enlistment: "Live bullets spinning past you aimed at sapping the life from your eyes will change your world in hurry. Breathe deeply. Slow and steady. Let your mind adjust and view these conditions as normal. The rest is in God's hands, my lad." Then his father presented Henry with his old field knife, which Henry now clutched tightly as the lighter inched closer to the shore. As fate would have it, Henry and his mates managed to land on the beach without a single casualty.

The beach itself was absolute pandemonium when the Dubs landed, not due to enemy fire as much as the result of lack of clear leadership. By noon, in the hundred-degree heat, the rough shoreline was crammed with thousands of dehydrated soldiers and stretcher-bearers racing about tending to any wounded soldiers. Most of the regiments were disorganized, with men still searching for their officers and NCOs. Henry, Connors, Brennan, McDonough, Shannon, and the other men of the 7th turned to junior officer Montgomery, expecting him to lead them on an advance inland towards the slopes of Lala Baba, but Montgomery simply stood on the beach dumbfounded.

"Lef-tenant. Should we advance?" Connors asked.

The young, pampered lieutenant stared back at him blankly, then briskly marched off in the direction of Major Dempsey.

"We ought to be advancing," hollered McDonough to Connors.

Montgomery stumbled towards Major Dempsey, saluting him. Dempsey quickly slapped the young lieutenant's hand.

"Damn it man, don't you listen? Every time you salute, you make us a target," Dempsey scolded the man.

"Apologies, sir. The men are requesting their orders. Do we advance?" Montgomery asked feebly.

"Have the men seek cover under the cliffs. Dig in and await orders," the major said in a firm tone. "Mr. Montgomery, remember, you are an officer in his Majesty's service—act like one."

Montgomery nodded repeatedly. He turned, lifted his chin, puffed out his chest as best he could, and marched towards the men.

"To the bottom of that cliff, you dogs," Montgomery snarled at the men as he unsheathed his well-polished sword and pointed it in the direction of the cliff. Montgomery charged past McDonough and ahead of the men into an untouched section of beach between the men of the 7th and the base of the cliff.

"You heard the lieutenant," Brennan said to the group, flinging his hefty kit bag over his shoulder.

Montgomery was about 40 feet away from them when he sensed that no one was on his heels obeying his order. He looked back over his shoulder and glared at the men. "Move!" he shouted, his voice cracking slightly, and he stomped his right foot forward and sliced the air with his sword. Just then an explosion of sand and rock erupted with a sound that could best be described as a hellish crack of thunder.

Pieces of Montgomery's body were sent high into the air in a pinkish red burst of flesh, fabric, and metal. The inexperienced officer had stepped directly onto a Turkish mine buried on the beachfront. The ghastly sight made Corporal Shannon buckle over and vomit into the sand.

Captain Gallager marched over to Shannon, grabbed him by his kit bag, and helped the man to his feet. "Take care not to make that a habit. If the bullets don't kill you, dehydration will," Gallager said.

"Sir," Shannon nodded.

"We are the 7th of Dublin," Gallager continued, making eye contact with the rest of the men. "We are the fiercest, bravest warriors to ever have blood pump through an Irish heart. Today is our day to show the world what mettle we are made of."

The captain's words prompted a bolt of adrenaline to surge through their veins. An aura of fearlessness radiated around the men. They were prepared to sprint across the beach when the captain raised his hand.

"And gentlemen, remember the Irish proverb: 'If you don't know the way, walk slowly,'" Gallager cautioned them with a daring glint in his eye. He then turned and proceeded to walk through the mine-laden beachfront.

The men rallied behind the captain's resolve. They followed him across the precarious sunbaked sand and rocks over to the safety of the base of the cliff.

On the other side of the beach, Barrington and Dempsey stared out at a landing craft that had run aground on a shoal off in the bay during the landing.

"This is a damn folly," Barrington grumbled to Dempsey.

"Sir, I will follow any order you give," the major responded.

"The general's only orders are to secure Suvla Bay and stay in reserve until all of our forces have been consolidated," the colonel continued to grumble.

"By nightfall, we won't have any forces left to consolidate if we let the enemy strengthen their defenses," the major suggested.

The colonel agreed with the major. The disdain he felt for Haultford, the lieutenant-general in charge of this operation, began to boil over, setting his Irish blood aflame. "They send an aged, peacock general with zero battle experience to lead this attack. It's a disgrace." The colonel snarled. "Follow me, Major."

Dempsey stayed close on the heels of the fuming colonel as they marched across the sweltering, congested beachfront and towards a signaling tent approximately 100 meters inland. Barrington swung the flap to the tent open forcefully and stormed inside. The colonel found several men seated around a wooden table set up with typewriters, message forms, signal flags, and telegraph equipment.

"Private," the colonel called out to Private Howards, a doe-eyed signaler who was tasked with sending and receiving wired communications from headquarters. "Send this message to General Hamilton." Barrington broke from protocol and decided to submit his evaluation over the head of Haultford and directly to the top.

The sapper paused and glanced at Barrington.

"General Hamilton," the colonel reiterated in a staccato tone.

The sapper readied his pencil and message form. "Go ahead, Colonel."

"General Hamilton. Men ashore. Beachhead secure. Golden opportunities are being lost. Requesting an immediate authorization to advance on weakened Turkish outposts. Colonel M. H. Barrington."

Howards took the message and rattled it off in Morse code across the telegraph line.

Henry and his mates fought off the swarm of flies in the afternoon sky and watched as a single artillery shell whistled above their heads and exploded with a scream into the bay about 10 meters away from them. A soldier from the 11th, wearing only his skivvies, dove into the bay and swam toward where the shell had erupted. The fresh-faced soldier dove under the water like a porpoise. After a few moments he returned to the surface with a large fish in his hands and grin upon his face, much to the dismay of McDonough, who watched on with a frown. The soldier jogged out of the water and tossed the fish at the feet of McDonough, who removed some money from his pocket and paid the lost wager.

"That money won't do you much good out here, mate," McDonough said sorely.

"No mate, but that fish will after you cook it for me," the soldier laughed.

McDonough removed his field knife and began to gut the fish.

"Supper will have to wait," said Captain Gallager as he approached the men. "Prepare to advance inland."

After an hour of having his men perform useless digging in the hard and rocky soil under the blazing sun, Colonel Barrington had had enough and elected to move his troops on an assault of the surrounding hills and join other regiments already engaged in fighting on Chocolate Hill. The colonel huddled around a map with his officers and gave them their final orders. "Mr. Murray and I will lead a regiment directly to Hill 53 and aide in its capture," the colonel commanded. "Major Dempsey and Captain Gallager, you will take a regiment of men to aide in the fight for Hill 10."

"Yes, sir," the men replied.

"For Ireland."

"For Ireland," the officers replied to the colonel with pride.

"God speed, gentlemen." The colonel placed the map

he was holding inside his tunic and marched off.

Henry listened intently as Dempsey swiftly delivered the men their orders while the rocky Aegean cliffs shielded them from back-to-back exploding artillery shells. "We will follow The Cut up and advance on Hill 10 from the south."

The Pals, under the leadership of Dempsey and Gallager, double-timed their way through the dry gully known as The Cut. The Cut was ripe with the stench of rotting flesh and sage. The pungent odor permeated Henry's nostrils, staining his senses. He was on high alert, and the silence found in the gully only increased the tension within the men. They had no idea what to expect, how many enemy troops lay ahead, where they were hiding, and what kind of firepower they had at their disposal. Henry tried to imagine the cool shade of the majestic trees of St. Patrick's Park on his face and replace the scent of rot with that of Irish wildflowers. Ahead of him was Dempsey, who exuded the steely grit of a veteran as he calmly led the men with speed through The Cut. The sounds of war grew louder and louder, growing in fervor as the men drew near Hill 10. Plumes of grey smoke dotted the horizon like hot air balloons rising. The men gripped their rifles tighter and sharpened their eyes like golden eagles scanning for rabbits.

Dempsey guided the men out of The Cut, and the isolated sand dune known as Hill 10 came into view. The area was occupied by soldiers from the 9th Lancashire Fusiliers and the 11th Manchesters. The 9th and 11th had advanced on the hill early in the morning and forced the small Ottoman defenses to retreat towards the enemy outpost near Chocolate Hill.

"You boys are late for breakfast," said a wryly sergeant from the Manchesters, who stood smoking a cigar.

"Where do you suppose we can have the opportunity to shoot at a Turk around here?" McDonough asked.

"They skirted back around the salt lake and up to Chocolate Hill. There's plenty of them held up there," the sergeant said as he took a long puff off the cigar.

"What do you chaps say we go lend them a hand?" Dempsey said to his men with a smile.

The Dubs unleashed a masculine rumble.

"You fellas should rest up. Have some water. There's some rations in the tent over there. This climate catches up with you when you least expect it," the sergeant cautioned them.

"We've been resting for months," Brennan replied as he turned with the rest of the men south toward the dry salt lake.

"Watch for enemy snipers, chaps," the sergeant said as a last word of caution.

The men worked their way through the soft mud around the dry salt lakebed in an easterly direction and then through a gully blanketed in dense, stunted oak and prickly holly bushes that rose up three to four feet. This was the perfect hunting ground for enemy snipers who loved to belly up next to the twisted bushes. The dark cloud of flies consuming the fallen in the distance confirmed this danger. Henry was at the front of the formation, blazing the trail through the thorny brush. His ears were perked and eyes keen, but an uneasiness continued to squash around in his guts. The sun cast shadows on the rocky terrain that every so often resembled a soldier lying prone on the ground.

Henry slowly moved a patch of collapsed, tangled brush out of his path with the tip of his bayonet. The brush was heavy and forced Henry to use his forearm to heave the branches back. As he passed through, the weight of the branches caused them to swing back on him; the thorns stung into his back, striking him across his kit pack and down along his unprotected flanks. He winced as the thorns pierced his khakis. In the field, with the diseased flies, limited antiseptic, and even less clean water, even the slightest abrasion could turn septic. Henry turned back to adjust the entrenching tool in his kit pack in an attempt to keep it from rubbing against his scratches and came face to face with a Turkish sniper. Henry yelled and thrust his bayonet into the man's chest before realizing the sniper was already dead. The lifeless sniper was disguised in foliage and green paint and propped up like a puppet spread eagle against a row of holly bushes. Henry dropped onto his rear to compose himself.

Gallager rushed to Henry's side with his revolver extended in front of him. Upon seeing the body of the deceased, the captain turned to Henry with a smile and said, "Better to be safe than sorry, ay, Calhoun?"

More men from the 7th emerged from the hedgerows. They looked about, finding themselves on the edge of a series of dry, plowed fields ripe with the remnants of war. One by one, the men stopped at the fields and searched for signs of the enemy.

McDonough came up to the front and stood beside his friend. "Henry, old boy, you seem to have located the source of the flies," he said in a charming lilt. McDonough reached his hand down to help Henry up.

Henry rose to his feet and took in the view of the field.

Fly-infested corpses covered the ground, swollen and bursting in the blistering sun. The silence was deafening. Were they about to walk into this quiet field and suddenly find themselves sawed in half with machine gun fire and artillery shells?

Dempsey worked his way to the front of the ranks and found Gallager. "Captain, your binoculars, please."

Gallager removed his binoculars and handed them to the major, who then walked over to a nearby dense oak. Dempsey took several cautious glances around the area and swiftly proceeded to scale the tree to the canopy. The major knew he would be completely exposed to enemy fire, but he was not about to send his men into a meat grinder. If the safety of his men meant risking his life for additional reconnaissance, then so be it. He brought the binoculars to his eyes and scanned the trench line across the fields and mountain line above. Fighting could be heard in the far distance but seemed contained to Chocolate Hill. Their path was clear. Dempsey worked his way back down the tree and, with a final leap, landed on the ground below where Gallager waited.

"You'll never plow a field by turning it over in your mind. Right, Captain Gallager?" Dempsey smiled, removing his revolver from its holster as he returned to the pack of men. "If the element of surprise is on our side, let's not squander it this time."

Dempsey trotted out across the fields toward the maze of trenches. Without a second thought, Henry and his band of mates followed suit. The men were hound like in their advance, with steely blood racing through their veins. If the enemy was to bleed the life from their young bodies on this day than they better have plenty of bullets on hand because the 7th was not going to be denied victory in their first fight of the war. The men reached the entrance to the well-constructed Turkish trenches near the base of Chocolate Hill without a shot fired.

"I'm beginning to feel we may never see action," McDonough quipped.

A long trench ran along the front line. It staggered, which kept anyone from seeing more than a few yards from their left or their right. A soldier's focus was to be on the battle ahead of him. The trench walls sloped inward as they descended into the depths of the trench, and they were lined with wood: everything from local saplings and cut trees to wooden crate planks to keep the earth from falling and filling in. The floor was lined with planks and kept clear of debris. Along the front wall of the trench, steps were constructed that housed ammunition boxes underneath. They also served as seats as men waited for battle. At the end of the long, winding trench, Henry came across what looked to him to be the entrance to a small mine shaft. The front line dugout entrance was lined with planks from crates to keep the walls from caving in. The steps into the dugout led Henry roughly five meters down. The dugout room was designed to protect some of the men from shelling. This particular dugout was just a rectangle carved from the earth large enough for ten men to stand in a huddle.

Henry made his way back toward the middle and turned to his right, down a sequence of trenches that led to a deep dugout which ran twelve meters into the ground. This dugout was large and would most assuredly survive shell fire.

The maze of trenches was all empty, but the smell of smoke in the air became stronger; they were close. An excitement raged in the men as they reached the base of Chocolate Hill. They arrived just in time to take part in the final advance on Chocolate Hill with several hundred soldiers from other Irish regiments and a number of troops from the 11th already engaged in heavy fighting.

A bullet struck the ground near McDonough and kicked dirt into his face. The private laughed. "This is what a battle should look like, mate," McDonough said to Henry.

Several hundred soldiers were already scaling the hill

and feeling the brunt of the Turkish war machine. Rockets exploded in all directions. Machine gun fire tore through the hearts of men barely old enough to love. This was a battle to the death. Men, young and old alike, cried out in pain as shrapnel cleaved limbs and bullets burst bellies wide open. The enemy retreated to the top of the hill, where they had a clear advantage. There the Turkish forces aimed their cannons and machine guns downhill and bombarded them, leaving the hill pockmarked with bomb craters and bodies. The time had come for the 7th to prove their might in a charge that would cause Chocolate Hill to be renamed Dublin Hill in their honor.

"Let our deeds prove as great as the deeds of the heroes who have given their lives before us! God save Ireland!" Gallager cried out as he waved a green flag that he had attached to the end of his sword. He drew his revolver and stormed up the hill.

The men of the 7th roared. The reply chants from his men—the heat from the fire of their breath—was strong like the rush of wind at his back that carried him towards the summit. The athletic Dubs charged behind their captain armed with bullets and sheer brawn. The Allied troops above found themselves startled at the tremendous sound from the Irish fighting force that overtook them and drowned out the sound of the cannon fire. The troops marveled at the tenacity, endurance, and sheer grit of the battle charge of the 7th. The Dubs were quite the sight to behold: avenging Irish angels or fire-breathing devils to the Turks, who watched in disbelief as these Irishmen charged gallantly through bullets and jagged shrapnel. When one man fell, another man charged ahead with even greater fervor at the sight of his lost brethren.

Major Dempsey was the first of the Dubs to reach the summit. He hollered, "Don't break the line! Carry on, men!" as a bullet ripped through his thigh. A blink later, Henry witnessed a second bullet tear through the major's cheek as the officer raised his revolver and fired. The shot was true, striking an advancing Turkish soldier in the chest. Then the stouthearted leader fell and crimsoned the soil.

The Allied troops rallied behind the major's last words and broke over the crest of the hill. Henry was able to see Captain Gallager wave his sword, the undeniable green flag raised high, as he disappeared over the crest of Chocolate Hill into the enemy's defenses.

Henry raced towards the peak. He could see Brennan several meters in front of him. A spark flew in Henry's eye from a bullet hitting the stones. He quickly wiped his eye with his sleeve. His under-eye singed and his vision blurred. Through the haze, he saw a Turkish grenade tumble from the sky and explode near Brennan, knocking the sergeant to the ground. Henry mustered his strength and rushed to Brennan's side. Brennan shouted angrily at being hit and clutched his stomach.

Henry lifted Brennan over his shoulder and carried him to the summit. The shelling fell silent. The Turkish forces retreated, being chased by the 7th and the 11th. All that was left were the dead bodies of their brothers and the Turkish defenders. Their forces had taken Chocolate Hill but at a great loss of life. Exhausted and dehydrated, Henry collapsed on the dark ground with Brennan.

"I'm worm meat, Henry," Brennan grimaced.

Henry applied pressure to Brennan's stomach wound. "Hang on. A stretcher-bearer will be here soon and take you off to get all fixed up," he said.

Henry knew the wound was fatal but continued to do his best to calm Brennan. He reached into his field jacket and removed a crushed pack of smokes. He took out a cigarette, lit it, and then placed the cigarette in between Brennan's chapped lips. Brennan took a deep drag and exhaled.

"Hey, old boy, you never told me why you were late to the ship in Alexandria?" Henry said, trying to take Brennan's mind off his injury.

Brennan smiled and began to chuckle. "I spent all I

had on a belly dancer. I never set out to. I was sitting in a tea house along Shatby Beach. I was enjoying a fine cup of tea and sheesha when this most beautiful woman, who had been sitting at the table behind me, stood to leave. She tapped me on the shoulder and told me in rough broken English that she needed an escort to walk her to where she was going to dance. Being the gentleman that I am, I offered the lady my elbow and took her to her club. She led me inside and sat me at a small round table for one in the corner, positioned between the stage and a staircase."

Brennan coughed and puffed again on the cigarette between his lips.

"The band came out and took the stage. Once the music began to play, she returned. I tell you she was the most luminous thing I've ever seen. She was covered from head to toe in gold shimmering pieces, and yet she appeared to be hardly dressed. The fabric that made up her dress must have been made from spider silk. You could see right through it. Her bits and pieces were covered, but just barely. To top off her outfit, she wore a candelabra with eight lit candles on her head. She walked carefully into the middle of the room and began to dance. She moved her hips and her belly in ways that you wouldn't think were possible. I swear, Henry, there were moments when you would think she didn't have any bones in her body at all. She dipped down low and sat on the floor with one leg in front of her and one leg behind. Then she jumped up high, and the candelabra on her head stayed in place and the candles all stayed lit. I tell you, Calhoun, it was the second most impressive thing I've ever seen."

"What was the most impressive?" Henry asked, trying to keep Brennan talking.

"The most impressive thing came later. At the end of her dance, she came to me. She took my hand and led me up the stairs to her room. She asked me to blow out the candles and help take the candelabra from her head. Then she poured a couple of brandies and she danced for me, privately. Every dance she did, more of her costume came off. For her last dance, she had me wet gold coins with my tongue and stick them to her skin. Then she would move and shake until all of the coins fell off. Then she...."

Brennan stopped himself for a moment. He considered the decorum of his conversation then he continued.

"She and I had what men and women around the world have every day. Only I think our encounter was better. It was simply wondrous."

"That doesn't sound half bad," Henry said softly.

"No, siree...not half bad...Henr...." Brennan's eyes

fluttered back in his head and then closed peacefully with a final exhale.

Henry grabbed the cigarette as it slipped from Brennan's lips and crushed it angrily in his palm. He made the sign of the cross with his thumb on his friend's forehead and placed his arm around Brennan's neck, embracing him. The shelling had stopped before the men reached the hilltop, but the scent of sulfur and burnt metal permeated the air. Henry gently laid his pal down, stood up, clenched his jaw, and went on to search the scarred hilltop for any other wounded soldiers.

Dead bodies were draped throughout the brushwood. Henry stepped near the body of Major Dempsey. Dempsey's sparkling blue eyes had turned black. His mask of determination had softened into a peaceful expression of neutrality. Henry kneeled beside the major and delicately closed the man's eyelids. Calhoun felt as though he had lost a second father. Tears flowed from his eyes as he said a prayer for his leader. Henry finished his prayer, wiped his eyes, and continued searching for survivors.

"So this is what victory looks like," Henry thought to himself as he slowly approached one of the abandoned Turkish Howitzers. The Howitzer was plated on the front and both sides. The side plating had an Arabic inscription painted on it that translated to "God is with us." Waves of thick smoke swept across the hilltop and over the gun.

Henry's eyes burned, and his nose watered from the fumes as he leaned over the side plating of the Howitzer to find an arm draped over the back end of the gun. The arm bore a cuff badge with three stars, signifying the rank of captain. Further up the uniform, on the blood soaked collar, was the distinct insignia of D Company, the 7th Royal Dublin Fusiliers: a grenade crowned with the tiger and elephant. Henry hurried around the gun to find the body of Captain Gallager. Gallager's sword was still clenched in his right hand, the green flag that was tied around the blade was now twisted all the way down to the hilt and drenched in blood. The length of the steel blade was thrust through the body of a Turkish gunner. Taking the officer for dead, Henry turned to step away from the Howitzer just when a low wheeze puffed out of the captain. He was still clinging to life. Henry rushed to the man's side, draped him over his broad shoulders, and used the last of his strength to lug the man to the safety of the hospital dugout.

Days passed with both sides locked in a chess match. The Allies would capture a ridge just long enough to run out of supplies and reinforcements before being driven back again by a new onslaught of Turkish forces. Night raids became commonplace—as did the dead bodies that racked up on the battlefield from the men who carried out the raids. One by one the men of the 7th were called to join their brothers with the Lord.

Deaglan Connors, the former coal miner, found himself caked in grease, clay, and dried blood as he crawled back with two other survivors from one such raid. The bullets had stopped and the night stood still. Henry, McDonough, and Shannon were the first to meet the men as they approached the front line trench to help pull them to safety. As the men leapt into the trench, Deaglan found himself the third man out. He crouched to spring into the protection of the trench, but as his legs launched him forward, a sniper gave the poor bloke a goodnight kiss, striking him through the back of the neck and severing his windpipe.

Henry, McDonough, and Shannon led the burial party for their friend the following morning. They gently hummed a verse from quartermaster Lloyd's hymn as their shovels pushed the rocky sand over Deaglan's wooden overcoat. Henry used his father's knife to clean up two thick branches and fastened them together into a simple cross to serve as a grave marker for the man. Next, he sharpened a point on the bottom of one of the beams and sank it deep into the sand to anchor the cross. Shannon took Deaglan's helmet and gently hung it on the top of the cross. The men stepped back, lowered their heads, and said a silent prayer. Henry made the sign of the cross, and the three men stared out towards the bay.

"It's peaceful when we don't have bombs going off around us. Nice and quiet," Shannon said, musing.

"It's only quiet because the bombs already made you deaf," McDonough snickered. Shannon stared straight ahead, unable to hear McDonough.

Henry put his arm around Shannon's shoulder. "It is a beautiful view, and hopefully one day these grounds will be covered in lush green grass to remind them of home."

"What's that?" Shannon said, turning to Henry.

"We have to get back to the trenches. The sun will be out in full force soon," Henry said and gathered his things to march back to the dugouts.

The brutal heat, incessant flies, and lack of clean water began to claim more casualties than the relentless bombings from the Turkish defenses. The Allied troops found themselves ravaged with dysentery, and the absence of clean water made it near impossible for the men to stave off dehydration. Henry was no exception. His intestines flamed and bathed his bowels in blood. Before the war, he felt indestructible, especially on the rugby pitch. The effects of war had quickly humbled him. The no man's land was no rugby pitch, and the players most certainly did not shake hands after a volley of cannon fire. Still, he did his best to keep a stiff upper lip, but every night and every morning he prayed for a reprieve—for the Turks to crack and run. But the Turkish forces held every advantage and nightly crept their front line closer and closer to the Allies. Their snipers merged with the brush in the no man's land and waited mercilessly for any of Henry's mates to dare cross in front of their rifle sights. In spite of this, the brass hats continued to send men again and again in acts of pure folly to try and claim control of the hills around Suvla Bay.

The springs and wells in the landscape remained hidden to the Allied forces, and the one's they discovered were soon poisoned by Turkish forces. The Turkish men used their expert knowledge of the landscape and the locations of fresh water to give them the upper hand while the men of Henry's regiment continued to succumb to thirst and dysentery. The Turkish forces exploited this illness, and by mid-August even the latrines were no longer safe. The Turks began targeting the waste facilities, knowing the soldiers would ultimately be forced to relieve themselves.

Henry lay in a fetal position in the dugout he shared with McDonough. His mouth was dry and his lips were badly chapped. He unsheathed his field knife and slowly used it to dig up a tin of water buried in the floor of the dugout. The men found that storing their water rations in sealed tins underground helped to prevent the water from evaporating in the scorching summer sun. Henry pried off the lid and slowly sipped the lukewarm fluid. Each gulp cramped his stomach. Unable to control his bowels, Henry climbed out of the dugout carved into the wall of the trench and rushed to the latrine several meters behind the line. The stench of the latrine would have most certainly been unbearable for Henry, but the incessant scent of gunfire, grease, and blood had already numbed his sense of smell.

The latrine was simply a ditch with boards laid across to sit down on. Henry found a frail private from the 11th hunched over the latrine with his eyes shut. Concerned the man might fall in, Henry went to pull him away from the latrine. Men on more than one occasion were known to fall in from exhaustion and had even drown in their own excrement. As Henry pulled the man forward, he felt the dead weight of the body. The Lord had already taken the private from this hell on Earth. Henry rolled the soldier on his side and went about taking care of his business.

War was many things, but courteous it was not.

After Henry let nature take its course, he located a field medic and sent him to collect the private. The private would be taken to the cemetery several miles behind the lines on the northern slopes, where Deaglan Connors rested in peace. Burial parties could be seen every evening and each morning working on the northern slopes, burying those who were lucky enough to die on their side of the line. The ferocity of the fighting was so intense now that the enemy only gave the Allied forces a short reprieve to retrieve their wounded and dead from the no man's land before launching another rocket attack. This left many dead and mortally wounded men abandoned where they fell.

Henry made his way back to his dugout and climbed into it to find McDonough preparing a meal. Henry sat down beside McDonough and rested his head against the dirt wall.

"Oy, Henry. I forgot to tell you, General Haultford was sacked. I overheard a lieutenant from the 11th blabbing on about it," McDonough said. "That old poodlefaker wasn't fit to lead a spit-and-polish parade."

"Doesn't matter much now unless the Turks crack. We're stuck in the thick of it. This position is indefensible for us, and they know it," Henry said as he swatted away a fly.

"How many you wager we are down?"

"Over half dead, probably more."

"Who is in command anyway with General Haultford gone?"

"The division commander."

"Nope. General Byron left the peninsula. Lieutenant said he heard the colonel say the general was upset over the lack of promotion."

"Coward. Demands we shoot our own men as punishment for desertion and he flees the battle over vanity," Henry said as he grasped his swollen guts in agony. "Well, we still have the colonel."

McDonough watched his rugged friend struggle to fend off the pain. "There's no shame in going to see the field doctor, Henry. They can get you on a boat for Mudros to recover. You have fought as bravely as any man out here. No one will think you a deserter."

"My place is here with you chaps," Henry said, taking a deep breath.

"If it wasn't for you, five chaps would have been burned alive on the other side of the line, no thanks to the stretcher-bearers. You've proved you're a hero, mate. Now it's time to get yourself healed up."

"I won't hear any more of it," Henry said politely.

McDonough noticed the loud sounds of the frogs croaking and locusts whistling. He peered out of the dugout. The wretched amphibians had made their homes in the puddles of brackish water leftover from wells the desperate soldiers had dug near the trenches in failed attempts to source fresh water.

"Ain't that the damnedest thing? Hardly a drop of fresh water in this cursed place and frogs everywhere. Frogs, flies, disease, hunger, thirst," McDonough said as he crouched back down. "I saw a rat eat the eyes from a dead sergeant of the 6th Munsters in the no man's land yesterday, Henry. The damn creature scurried right past the man's pack where a tin of bully beef was poured out, shot to pieces. I swear the foul creature just turned up its nose at the tin and went straight for the poor chap's face. It's a helluva sight when rats don't even fear us," McDonough continued half joking. "They were right. This is the war to end all wars. It's the end of days."

"You aren't getting afraid are you, mate?" Henry teased.

"No fears," McDonough said as he used a biscuit to scoop up his dinner of bully beef, which he had warmed in a tin, turning it into a sludgy, corned-beef stew. Warming the beef served two purposes: the sludge helped soften the tooth-cracking biscuits, and the temperature helped kill the foul taste just enough to make it barely edible.

Henry stared up into the sky as night began to set in. Through the bellowing clouds of artillery smoke, the north star shone brightly. "Have you ever looked up in the sky and thought to yourself how amazing it really is that as humans we have the ability to understand how small we really are in this world? That God gives us the ability to see beyond this world? It's quite humbling, and here we sit fighting over a hill of dirt."

McDonough chewed his stinky beef-soaked biscuit and reconsidered Henry's question. "There is one thing. I don't think I was aware of it until those Turkish bastards blew off McAllister's clackers with a grenade. Have you ever noticed that whenever we charge into battle, we all sort of lean forward a little more than usual? You know, instinctually to protect our bollocks. That would be my—second—greatest fear. To have my bollocks blown to bits."

"What would be your first?"

"My gal Johanna leaving me because I had my bollocks blown to bits," McDonough chuckled.

McDonough meant what he said, but even still, he couldn't help but release a laugh. Henry joined him. The men continued to laugh so hard that Henry's eyes began to weep. He wiped at his face with his sleeve and clutched his guts, trying to maintain his sense of continence.

"What do you fear most, Henry?" McDonough asked.

"I used to think it was not being able to spend the rest of my life with Deirdre."

"Fitzpatrick? Deirdre Fitzpatrick?"

"Yea."

"Oh, mate, you were lucky she left you. That was a blessing from the good Lord above."

"Why would you say a thing like that?"

"I'm not about to break your heart while we sit stuck in a rotting trench. And you, with your bowels having a mind of their own and all, who knows what might happen. Just trust me."

Henry sat uneasy, taunted by the information McDonough was refusing to relinquish.

McDonough gave Henry a long, hard look. "You really want to know, mate?" he said, seeing the sorrow in Henry's eyes.

"Yes," Henry answered.

"I heard she was with child from that plonker she ran off with. She was afraid her parents would have her committed to a work house. So she ran off. Sorry, but, there you go."

Henry sat back, feeling somewhat relieved at the news. After a moment, he said with a cheery face, "Well, she did the right thing then."

"She the reason you ran off on this great adventure?"

"I suppose, partly. In that regard I am no different from many of the other fellas out here."

"You are right about that. Many a man has the image of a good, Irish bure embedded in the back of his skull. Most believe I am fighting this war because I have the temperament for it. To tell you the truth Henry, I'm fighting this war for her." McDonough took a picture of Johanna out of his breast pocket and handed it to Henry to have a look. "She's doing clerical work in a hospital."

"The Lord modeled a fair piece of clay, mate. Maybe I ought to hang on to this?" Henry went to place the picture in his own breast pocket.

"Hey, hand it over. And don't be getting any ideas. I plan on making it out of this war, bollocks intact."

"McDonough. Calhoun." A firm voice rang out near their dugout. The voice belonged to Lieutenant Murray, the last of their officers. The once young-looking lieutenant now had the signs of a man who had aged ten years in a week. The fighting had turned him into quite the leader, and the men were honored to serve alongside him. He peered his war-wrinkled face into the dugout. "We're on the move. The chaps from the 31st are under heavy fire on the ridge near Kidney Hill, and command refuses to order a withdrawal."

"7th to the rescue," McDonough said as he hurried to eat his last biscuit.

"Calhoun, you should sit this one out," the lieutenant said as he watched Henry grimace and struggle to his feet.

"You need someone to be your guardian angel, sir." Henry cracked a half smile.

"Bring up the rear then," the lieutenant said simply.

Henry nodded, reached for his rifle, and followed McDonough and Murray down the trench to gather the other men.

Murray led a force that included McDonough, Shannon, and Henry and about a dozen or so other men who had been patched together from various units. They snaked through their trench, past the Allied encampment of Jephson's Post until they reached the front line and prepared to be spit out at the base of Kidney Hill. The shifting sand of the dunes trembled beneath Henry's feet from the constant pounding of artillery. The air was ripe with a symphony of wind instruments of war. The full might of the grim reaper's baton was on display. Soldiers on both sides of the line cried out as bullets and shrapnel made mincemeat of the men.

The Turkish soldiers had positioned themselves on the southern slopes as they fought the Allies for control of

78

the northern boundary of Suvla Bay, a ridge known as the Kiretch Tepe Sirt. From that position, the Turks lobbed grenades and fired rockets over the crest of the ridge and onto the men of the 6th, trapping them under a canopy of modern brimstone. Henry watched the rocket fire eat away at the steep, shrub covered slopes. The only way to slow the Turkish attack and provide support to the 6th was to cross an open plain that lay at the feet of Kidney Hill. Unfortunately for Henry and his mates, this open plain provided clear visibility for the Turkish artillery leaving the pals dangerously exposed.

Murray swallowed hard and was the first to go over the top and into the no man's land. In a wave of green, the remaining men joined suit as they charged towards the hill. Grenades and shelling swept the plain and hillside, striking four of the men before they reached the slopes of the hill. The heat of the shrapnel and explosions set the thick shrub of the open plain on fire behind the men.

Murray reached the base of the slope first and raged up it. The rock was loose and he suddenly lost his footing on the steep slope, hitting the deck hard. He winced, blood running from a cut near his eye. He dug in his heels and pushed forward. A Turkish grenade bounced on the ground near his feet. He quickly scooped it up and lobbed it back towards the summit, where it exploded.

Henry spotted the dark outline of enemy snipers against the orange bursts of grenades. He aimed his rifle and squeezed the trigger. Unable to confirm his hit, Henry continued his pursuit up the sharp slope. The fire raged behind him and ate away the darkness. With a wall of fire to their backs and the only live bodies in front of them belonging to the enemy, Henry and his pals knew there would be no retreat in this battle. So the men pressed forward into the gnashing teeth of the Turkish line.

Murray, followed by Shannon and several men, elected to change course and rush the hill up a steep path that was clear of burning brush. Soon that route became drenched in blood. Henry watched in horror as Murray took a bullet through his heel before a machine gun rendered him unrecognizable. Henry fired several shots in the direction of the machine gun fire and then sprinted for a crater in the hillside. He dove into the hole just as the machine gun sprayed a volley of gunfire towards his last position. This gave Shannon and another soldier on the steep path a momentary reprieve to break for cover. Shannon and the other soldier sprinted for the seaward slope known as the Pimple.

Henry carefully scanned the hillside for other men from his unit. The remainder of the men were following

Shannon towards the Pimple. Henry was alone and trapped in the crater. The only positive news was the apparent change in direction of the Turkish forces, who gave chase and focused their attack back on the northern slopes. Henry's heart rate slowly settled, and his ears adapted to the noise. Through the gunfire, he heard a weak voice call out to him: "Henry. Henry."

Henry slide his face against the ground and peered out from the crater to find McDonough lying wounded, several feet from the crater.

"Are you badly hit?" Henry whispered.

"More or less," McDonough replied.

"Splendid," Henry said wryly. He then rapidly grabbed his friend by the upper body and pulled him into the shelter of the crater.

McDonough's left leg was clinging to the rest of his body by his shredded thigh muscle and exposed tendons. His thigh bone was completely splintered, severing the femoral artery. McDonough had jammed his fingers into his upper thigh and was pinching the artery with all his might to stave off the bleeding.

Henry quickly detached his rifle sling from the rest of the weapon, hoping to use it as a field tourniquet. He pulled the sling high up on McDonough's leg, near his groin, and struggled to tighten it deeply between

McDonough's groin and hip. Henry removed his bayonet from his weapon and slipped it through the sling, using it as a lever to tighten the tourniquet.

"At least I still have my bollocks, pal." McDonough grinned before choking for breath.

"Jephson's Post isn't far off. Hang on, Robert. I'm getting you out of this."

Henry cautiously slid his face up out of the crater, cheek hugging tightly to the rocky ground. He glanced south in search of a clear path, but the brush behind them was still in flames. He tilted his head north. At that moment, a bullet struck the rocky ground in front of him, sending a spark flying into his forehead. Henry wiped the cinder and stared to the north, beyond the bodies of both rotting and newly fallen soldiers. In the flashes of exploding grenades, he was able to make out the remainder of his regiment. They had managed to push through to the northern slopes, but Henry would never make it that far with McDonough. Henry's only option was to race McDonough over to a dangerously steep slope southeast of them, navigate their way down, and then follow a maze of gullies back to the field hospital at Jephson's Post.

Henry watched and waited for a moment as the Turkish forces turned their full attention back to the troops north of them. His chance had come. Henry slid back into the crater and turned to McDonough. McDonough was breathing in hefty, staccato bursts as his hands trembled to unbutton his breast pocket.

"Time to go, Robert," Henry said.

McDonough shook his head and pointed repeatedly to his breast pocket, as if his finger were a woodpecker's beak. Henry leaned into the man and helped him unbutton his pocket. McDonough pulled at the open pocket with his right index finger.

"I'll get it, mate," Henry said as he delicately removed the photograph and placed it in between McDonough's fingers.

McDonough looked lovingly upon Johanna's picture. The rhythm of his breath slowed, and the heavy, staccato panting turned into slow, drawn out sighs.

"We have to go, mate. Now's our chance," Henry urged.

"The loves of our lives are the only significant things in this world, Henry." McDonough reached out his left hand and gently patted Henry on the cheek.

Henry watched as McDonough's hand drifted from off his cheek down to the rocky soil and his body sank, heavy with death. Rage welled up inside of Henry as he gently shut his dear friend's eyelids. He clasped his rifle, mustered his courage, and climbed out of the hole to follow after his regiment. In that moment, a sniper's bullet seared through his chest, followed by another round, and another. Henry stumbled forward for several steps until a fourth round split his midsection, singeing a path through his swollen guts and effectively stopping Henry in his tracks. He collapsed. The air fell silent as his mind registered the severity of his situation. The pain was surprisingly absent as endorphins flooded his nervous system. Henry's eyes rolled to the back of his head, and his senses fell silent.

Time stood still and Henry lay awaiting his fate. The flash of light and heat on his face from the bombs bursting in battle faded. The fighting had ceased. As the minutes drifted away, Henry heard the gentle sound of rocks crunching under foot.

"There's too many. We can't get them all, sir," an Allied medical orderly said while he and a medical officer set a stretcher down on the ground.

"Take the ones that can be saved and tag them. Leave the rest for the Almighty," the medical officer instructed.

The field ambulance unit only had a short window to salvage who they could, and they briskly went about the business of sorting the living from the dead or soon to be dead. The men who had a shot at life received the only priority. This was the cold reality of war.

Henry lay still in the no man's land, unable to speak, the life seeping out of the wounds in his body as he stared up into the starlit abyss. The medical orderly hiked his way in the vicinity of Henry. The orderly was so close Henry felt the ground vibrate with the man's steps. Would the orderly take pity on Henry and at least carry him off for a proper burial? Or would he simply leave him here for the sun to scorch him and the flies to feast on him? Henry watched, his vision going in and out of focus, as the orderly glanced at his wounds.

The orderly rolled Henry over onto his right side and inspected his exit wounds. As Henry's head fell to the side, he saw the rows of the charred remains of his fallen brothers. The orderly turned Henry back onto his back, made the sign of the cross with his thumb on Henry's forehead, and walked away.

The night fell silent. The field was desolate, and the temperature had dropped. Henry prayed silently to himself and hoped that God was free for a few seconds to listen. *My time has come, Lord. Please be merciful in your judgment and forgive my trespasses.* Henry closed his eyes. He felt as though his body were floating inches above the ground. Weightlessness and the cool caress of the nighttime breeze overtook his body as his mind pictured a wash of blue. As Henry drifted out of consciousness, he felt as though his body had begun to rotate and spin on an axis, still floating inches above the ground, all awhile being blanketed by a fog of blue mist. The light touch of the blue mist was comforting and cool. The light blue cloud slowly wafted all around his floating spinning body until he was fully covered in the blanket of comfort.

Hours later, in the dead of night, a cold wisp of air sent a shock through Henry's system, snapping him back into consciousness. He trembled. His khaki uniform was stiff with blood. He began to think about his mother and his father: their well-being without him, the promise he had made to return his mother's locket, and the disappointment he would cause his father when they learned of his death. Henry's resolve began to fortify. He refused to rot on this hillside.

He stared up at the night sky, confident with his chances for survival. Henry slowly moved his fingers, making sure they would follow his commands. He repeated the task with his elbows, knees, ankles, and toes. He seemed to be in remarkably good working order for someone who had been shot several times. There was weakness in his muscles however. Though his movements were slight, Henry noticed the considerable effort that was put into completing each task. As he continued to stare up into the star-filled blanket of darkness, he slowly rolled his head to the right. His head felt heavy, but his muscles were still obeying his command. He then turned his head to his left. That's when he saw it.

Henry felt his pulse quicken. His spirits were suddenly lifted. The ridge was within his sight. The top of the hillside that separated him from a downhill descent to the trenches where his Allied mates were surely held up for the night was merely yards away. Henry raised his right arm and crossed it over his body. He grabbed a handful of grass and tugged at it, pulling himself onto his side. Pain shot through his body as he lay on his side staring at the crest of the hill that would surely lead him to safety and life-saving assistance. He regained his strength and repeated the task until he rolled himself onto his belly. Henry rested on his belly for a moment, flicking grains of sand away from his left eye with his eyelashes as he blinked. His breathing became labored. He felt wetness as his blood began to pool underneath his body. Henry swallowed hard and began to make the painful laborious journey toward the ridge.

With his arms stretched out before him and all of the strength he could muster, Henry dug his fingers into the ground and pulled himself a few inches forward. He reached out and repeated the motion, gaining only inches with each pull. He clawed at the brush around him. The holly needled his hands as he pulled his body toward the steep path that swerved up the hill. He set his focus on the edge of hill. If he could reach the incline, he would tumble down the hill, closer to the front line. Hopefully someone would see him and alert a medic to his presence. The no man's land was no more than ten meters in some places. Henry was running on pure will. He slithered his body inch by grueling inch. He was close now; the slope was only a couple feet away. He pushed off the ground; his chest pounded with pain as he lifted his torso off the ground and lunged at an angle, tucking his chin with his head pointed downward. His shoulder hit the steep area, and gravity did the rest. Henry tumbled end over end until he landed hard on his back at the bottom of the hill. His body twisted and cracked its way, crashing into burnt brushwood below.

Only feet from the trench, Henry thought to himself, *Surely, one of my mates had to have heard my fall.*

"Ambulance," he cried out faintly. Henry was surprised at how faint his voice sounded compared to the amount of effort he was putting into being heard. It felt to him that he was screaming at the top of his lungs, yet he could barely even hear himself.

The battle had claimed over seventy percent of the forces who charged the hill. The remaining soldiers had abandoned the trench to help carry the wounded to makeshift field hospitals. No one was there to hear his cries. As Henry's heartbeat faded, a black clothed figure appeared in the darkness. *Is it a Turk? Did he somehow hear my faint cry for help? Has he come to put me out of my misery with a quick thrust of his bayonet?* Henry left himself to God's hands saying softly, "Your will be done." His eye lids closed leaving him in darkness to die. Henry's consciousness left him and this time all was silent, dark and still.

Henry woke from what felt to him to be a very long sleep to find himself lying on his back looking up at a high-arched ceiling with the scene from Christ's crucifixion painted upon it.

"Where am I? How long have I been unconscious? I was shot," Henry muttered.

The round, kind-looking face of a man in his early twenties came into Henry's view, blocking it from the painted ceiling above him. The man cupped the top of Henry's head in his strong hand and brought his face closer, examining Henry's eyes for consciousness. The man had short-cropped black hair. His eyebrows and light scruffy beard matched the color and texture of the hair on his head exactly. His dark brown eyes showed the depths of a soul bathed in kindness. His olive-toned skin ran smooth across the man's face, broken by two plump pink lips that curved into a slight smile.

"Rest," the man whispered into Henry's ear as he wrung the water out of a small cloth and began to dab Henry's brow. "You are not fully recovered yet. The love of Christ is healing you, but it is a slow process. You must rest."

Henry began to rise, but the pain that shot through his chest and right side brought him quickly back to the flat of the table he was lying on.

"Please, rest," the man said.

"I have to get back to my unit," Henry said.

"The fighting is far away from you now," the man said. His English was slightly broken, with a thick Turkish accent. "Father Keshishian brought you here. This is a place of safety. You were badly wounded when he found you. I believe you were left to die. My wife, Elina, was tasked with looking after you, but she is very pregnant with our first child and she can no longer attend to you. My name is Davit. Now that you are awake, I must alert Father Keshishian. Please, do not move from this altar until I return with him."

Henry watched as the young man dropped the cloth into a wooden pail on the stone floor and quickly left the room by stepping through a small doorway cut into the stone wall, roughly two feet above the sloping floor. It was at that moment that Henry realized that he was in a cave. He closed his eyes and drifted off to sleep again.

The next time Henry woke, he felt a sharp pain in his left side. He opened his eyes to find Davit and another man examining fresh bandages wrapped around Henry's abdomen. Henry looked down the length of his body and saw the bandage wrap that started just below his strong chest and wound around his body to just below his waist. Brown woolen trousers had replaced his uniform pants, covering Henry from his waist to his ankles. Henry pulled himself upright and sat on the edge of the table, letting his feet find the dirt floor beneath him.

"How do you feel?" a white-haired man with olive skin and kind brown eyes asked.

"I would say that I feel like a man who's been shot, but for some reason, I feel more like a man who's been run down by a truck," Henry replied.

"Ah, a man of humor!" The white haired man laughed. "I'm Father Keshishian. I went to the Allied front to ask the soldiers to come to my village to help my people, but all I found was death. The day I found you, the Allied forces had retreated, and you were all but dead. I brought you to this place of refuge, where this small but devout group of Armenians fled during the Meds Yeghern."

"I can't thank you enough, Father." Henry said. "I must get back to my unit as soon as I can."

Henry ran his hand along his belly and side. He remembered being ripped apart by bullets, but the pain he expected to feel had faded. He tried to stand up from the table. A wave of dizziness came over him for a moment. Davit reached out and held Henry by the shoulders, steadying him until the dizziness subsided.

"Please, you should stay on the altar," Davit pleaded.

"I'm well enough to stand," Henry said as he took a single staggering step from the table he had been lying on without falling. "I'm well enough to get back to my mates." Henry staggered a bit and leaned back onto the table. He gave Davit a glance of admittance to his folly and sighed. "How's your wife, Davit?"

Davit gave Henry an angry glare, and then he turned and walked out of the room.

"Davit's wife Elina died during childbirth I'm afraid. His son Arsen is healthy and alive, I am happy to say."

"I'm sorry to hear that," Henry said. "Yesterday he

told me his wife was pregnant, and I thought...."

"It was not yesterday," Father Keshishian interrupted, "You have been here for quite some time. You have fallen in and out of consciousness upon the altar of our small chapel. Davit's son is healthy and Elina is in heaven. And you need to finish healing before you go."

"I appreciate the help. I owe you my life, but I must get back to my unit." Henry stood again and took a few steps away from the table.

"I will help you return to your Allied forces, but you do need more time to heal. Let's start with a short walk to the mets senyak, where we should find some food."

Henry and the white-haired priest walked slowly through a maze of candlelit caverns carved in the dolomite and made their way to a large room where several people were congregating along long tables. At the entrance to the room, Father Keshishian took two wooden bowls and spoons from a table and led Henry to a table where, soon after they were seated, a woman came with a bowl of stew and a ladle. She filled the men's bowls and left.

"In my village, they began by targeting the strongest hay men through conscription into the Ottoman Army. Soon, they drafted all of our men, some as young as fifteen and others as old as sixty," Father Keshishian began as the men ate.

Henry initially surmised the story Father Keshishian was relaying simply to be about a political crusade being brought down on the Armenian people—a casualty of war, he thought. He would discover Father Keshishian's accounts revealed something far worse than a fight for land or anything he or his mates were fed from the British army.

"Earlier this year," Father Keshishian continued, "the Turkish government began disarming the men forced into the army and placing them in labor battalions, where they are being murdered. On April 24th, many of us were arrested in Constantinople: teachers, doctors, officials, and clergy, including Father Balakian. This spread throughout the country. Thousands were taken and did not live to see another sunset. After Red Sunday, I came here and began to form a resistance: mostly from men in hiding, those who refused to become Turkish conscripts, others who deserted the military to escape the labor camps—anyone sympathetic to our plight. Turkish forces have continued raiding our cities, one by one, calling for a complete relocation of the remaining women and children from Hayastan, stating it is for their safety. Many are not making it out of the cities alive. Some have been sold into slavery, others raped and killed by Kurdish bandits as they fled. The soldiers are turning our sacred sites into ungodly pyres, locking women and children inside our churches and setting them on fire."

"Are there others like you fighting, or is this it?" Henry asked.

"There are others. In Musa Ler, and elsewhere. Some have joined the Russians to fight. This was not the first time the Ottoman government sought to murder our people, but I fear the bloodshed will not stop. Others have lost hope.

Believe me when I say this to you: we have fields of blood worse than anything you will ever witness on a soldier's battlefield. I once came across a tobacco field on the edge of a forest. Bodies were...bodies were dismembered as if the devil himself led a battalion of butchers across the countryside. I spotted a woman in the distance. She was hunched over what looked to be another body. When I approached the woman, I saw a silver necklace in the palm of her left hand and a bloody, sickle-shaped knife in the other. I cried out to her, 'You've butchered your neighbor.' She looked at me and screamed for help. This Turkish woman screamed for help for fear of me. I ran before she could have the local police upon me. That woman had been scouring the dead, cutting them open searching for treasure. The official government notices claimed Armenians had two weeks to clear their homes. When the soldiers came, people had only seconds to evacuate before their homes and all of their possessions were seized. That left some people to swallow their valuables. In this case, a silver necklace. In the dark, thieves break into houses, but by day they shut themselves in; they want nothing to do with the light." The father finished quoting Job 24:16.

Several days passed as Henry continued his recovery. His walks with Father Keshishian grew in length and frequency over the days. One day, before their walk, Henry stood in the small chapel that had been converted into his recovery room. Father Keshishian came to meet him.

"I cannot thank you enough for saving me, Father. But there is one thing that has been on my mind," Henry said.

"Ask your question," Father Keshishian said.

"I was shot several times. I've been in and out of consciousness and I have healed to where there's barely a scar, all of which is remarkable. But the most remarkable part is that I don't recall seeing a doctor. I've met you and a few others here, but none who have acted in the capacity of a medical person."

Father Keshishian pulled back the sheets from the

altar Henry had been using as a bed. Four large black stones were placed at the corners for the table to lie upon. The table top itself was a hand-planed olive wood top, roughly the size of a door. Two long wooden beams crossed each other in an "x" pattern, running diagonally from one corner to the opposing one. The spaces between the long planks were filled with smaller hand-hewn planks that were lashed together. Finally, plank wood trimmed the edges of the table framing it.

"You've been lying on Christ's cross," Father Keshishian revealed to Henry. "This ancient underground city has been here for a very long time, Henry. The treasures protected here are not only those who walk and talk within its walls."

"I'm forever in your debt for healing me, Father."

"God healed you, Henry."

"There must be a way we can contact the Allied forces," Henry said. "You've told me that we are in Thrace, near the western side. Why not take your people and the altar and flee into Greece? You are close on this side of the country," Henry pleaded.

The white-haired priest returned the cloth sheet to its proper place on the altar. He lit two lanterns, and the two men began to walk again. This time they took a different tunnel. Henry could tell by the incline of the tunnel floor that they were heading down, deeper into the earth.

"Down here in the darkness of this ancient city, we do God's work to restore the light. I have seen the horrors of the war you are fighting and beyond, but I have also witnessed the miracles of life through God's glory, including the miracle of your recovery."

"Let me help you get these people and your treasures to my regiment. We can get you all to safety."

"I was on my way to your commanders to seek aid when I came upon you. Mr. Calhoun, most of your brothers in arms are dead, wounded, or have withdrawn from Gallipoli. We are on our own and must protect what is greater than us. Not only are we protecting the wounded and the persecuted, but we are protecting treasures of religious and historical significance. My order has protected these for centuries."

The two men stopped in front of a small entryway blocked by a stone boulder. Father Keshishian set his lantern on the ground and rolled the boulder to one side, revealing a large room with shelves and urns within.

"Some treasures were taken and saved from the great libraries of Alexandria in the third century," he said as he led Henry into the chamber. "Others, like the table on which you lay at night have been touched by the Lamb of God, Jesus Christ himself."

Father Keshishian held his lantern up for Henry to see the scrolls on the shelves and in the urns all around the room.

"There are other treasures to protect that cannot fall into Turkish hands. My order has been protecting their secrets and their whereabouts for centuries. If we die, so will these treasurers from God. Hidden safe underground." Father Keshishian reached for a scroll wrapped in a leather case that was embellished with circular gold studs. "The secret knowledge held within these artifacts is much too precious to fall into the wrong hands. Would you believe me if I told you that inside this case rests a codex that contains the key to unlocking a cipher, foretelling the name of the future antichrist?"

"Before I woke up down here, probably not. Why are you trusting me with this information? Aren't you worried I might prove to be a thief?"

"I believe God has entrusted you to me, Henry. For what purpose, I do not fully know. But I trust God will reveal that in his proper time."

As the two men left the chamber and continued down through the tunnels, Henry noticed multiple tunnels intricately carved into the dolomite leading in multiple directions.

"People have sought refuge in these tunnels over the

centuries, during troubled times." The priest continued, "These corridors are carved deep underground into the tuff of the mountain with special air shafts. Down this corridor ahead, you will find a tunnel with fresh water flowing. We have all we need. You'll be safe in here."

"What if there are bombings from above?" Henry asked as he marveled at the construction of the city around him.

"We are all in God's hands." The priest smiled gently as they turned a corner leading to their final destination. They passed a large, round stone to their right blocking an entrance, similar to the one the priest had shown Henry a few minutes before. Henry could not help but wonder what lay behind that stone dam. Several meters down the corridor, Henry noticed a soft haze of lamplight pouring out of an arched entrance.

Henry's curiosity as to the contents of the stone-guarded chamber churned within him. He was like a school boy who was experiencing his first circus. Just to the left of the large stone, Henry noticed an opening. The stone had not been returned to its proper place the last time it had been moved. There was a space, not quite tall enough for the men to walk through without ducking their heads, but it was enough for the men to duck down and enter the chamber. Father Keshishian stepped through the entryway and disappeared inside. As Henry slowly followed the priest into the chamber, he peered back at the stone door. Having miscalculated his bend, at six foot two, Henry took a solid crack right on the crown.

Henry clutched the top of his head and winced. His sight turned to a black canvas with silver speckles floating all around. After a couple moments, the fuzziness dissipated and his sight came back into focus on a room approximately five meters wide and six meters deep. In the center of the far wall, a cross was carved into the tuff. A white, cloth-covered altar stood in front of it. The high, arched ceiling had hand-painted figures of the twelve disciples, and at the far end of the room, a painting Henry recognized. The room glowed a warm honey tone from the linseed oil lamps that rested on small shelves, which were also carved into the walls around the room. Henry was back in the chapel that served as his recovery room.

The next day, Henry lit a lantern and prepared to take a walk through the cavernous tunnels on his own. Davit had brought Henry a clean shirt and trousers to wear. Henry dressed and set out on a walk, following the path he and the priest had taken the previous day.

Henry explored the corridors of the underground city. He went to the room with the scrolls and urns. He took up his lantern and explored the room. Against the far back wall, Henry saw a row of clay jars, each roughly waist high. Some of the scrolls were rather large, while some were no larger than Henry's pinky finger. After hearing Father Keshishian's tales, Henry's curiosity had only grown and grown especially regarding the codex. He cautiously reached for the small leather case containing the codex and took it in his hands. He was examining an emblem engraved on one of the gold studs that appeared to be that of a slaughtered lamb, when he felt the room shake. Dust fell from the ceiling of the small room as Henry realized the cave system was being bombed. A second explosion from above the underground city caused several of the clay jars to tip over and crack open. Henry stuffed the codex inside his shirt. He left his lantern on the floor and dashed through the opening as the round stone crashed forward, blocking the room's opening and narrowly missing Henry's leg in the process. He ran down the corridor back toward the small chapel, hoping to find an exit. Screams echoed through the caverns as Henry searched the rooms along the corridor for a way out.

Another bomb shook the walls of the cave. Henry heard gunshots echoing through the underground city. He turned and ran down the ancient corridor and saw the large stone that covered the side entrance to the chapel. He grabbed his belongings from the neatly placed pile he had left them in on the top of the altar. He removed the cloth sheet and tried to lift the table from its stone resting place in an effort to hide the table that contained the true cross of Jesus Christ. The table would not budge. Henry was not strong enough to move the large wooden rectangle from its stone anchors. He heard more screams and gunfire. The invaders were getting closer. Henry turned to run, but his belt had become caught on a piece of metal protruding from one of the table's long crossed planks. He tugged and pulled at the leather, but it would not budge. Henry took out the knife his father had given him and was about to cut into the leather of the belt to free himself when he noticed the nail wiggled slightly within the wood. Henry stuck the tip of the knife into the wood next to the nail and used the knife to pry the nail out of the table. Once the nail was free from the table, it fell loose from Henry's belt and landed in the palm of his hand. Henry examined the nail for a brief second. He knew the nail within his hand was exceedingly old, and he thought that it may even date back to the time of Christ's death. If this table was truly constructed with Christ's cross, then this could be one of the nails used in his crucifixion. Henry saw the tip of the nail had broken away and was lying separately in his hand. He opened the locket he wore around his neck and placed the tip of the nail within it for safe keeping. The rest of the nail was large enough; Henry placed it into the front pocket of his trousers.

He ran down the corridor and found it came to a dead end, except for a hole in the ceiling, allowing water to flow down through a hole below his feet and through a channel barely large enough for a person to squeeze through, but Henry knew he had no other choice. He climbed down into the chilled water trough. Henry held his breath as he ducked his head underwater and swam beneath the wall. The four feet Henry had to swim under the stone wall until he came out in the next chamber seemed like an eternity to him. He came up for air in a narrow cavern. The water rose to his stomach as he worked his way down the channel. The walls around him became tighter and tighter as the water rose higher and higher. Henry made his way through the narrow crack in the mountain until the water's current picked up. The floor sloped down, becoming more forceful, almost knocking Henry off his feet. He pressed his palms firmly against the walls to either side to catch himself and then, one step at a time, he bounced himself slightly off the floor, allowing the current to carry him. Henry saw a sliver of light ahead of him as he rode the current away from the bombing and the gunshots.

Henry was barely able to fit through the narrow opening in the mountainside; his face scraped the rock wall as he was spat out and dropped ten feet straight down into a pool of water that turned into a small mountain river. The pool Henry landed in was surrounded by large rocks. Henry swam over to one of the lower boulders and held onto it as he caught his breath.

Henry pulled himself out of the water and onto one of the rocks. He looked to the hillside on his left and saw smoke rising into the air, accompanied by the thunderous booming of mortar rounds as they pelted the earth above the underground city. Henry turned his gaze to his right and saw the once-beautiful, now-decimated hillsides and the wasteland of war that sprawled to the west and into more mountainous territory. He knew he had to move carefully if he were to get back to his unit alive.

Henry rolled to his right side, lowered himself off of the large rock he had been lying on, and took refuge within its shade. He took a look at the sun, a sight he hadn't seen for some time. He then estimated the time of day to be mid morning based on the sun's position and the size and direction of the shadows of the rocks he was resting under. Henry then crawled out from the shelter of the rocks and lay on his belly in the sandy earth. The warmth of the sun on his back reminded him how unforgivingly hot the day could become; however, the temperature was much cooler than what Henry had expected. The air was cool, and to Henry, it even smelled as though it might rain. He took out his knife and jabbed it into the ground so that the hilt stood straight up, pointing at the sky. Then Henry took his finger and made a mark on the ground at the far edge of the shadow line the knife made. Henry then crawled back to the safety of the rocks and waited what he thought was about fifteen or twenty minutes. He then crawled out to the knife, observed the shadow on the ground, and made another mark at the new edge of the knife's shadow. He pulled the knife out of the ground and laid it between the two marks he had made. Henry knew that this would position the tip of his knife pointing west: the direction he needed to go in order to find territory not occupied by the Central Powers.

Henry headed west through Thrace and into Greek Macedonia. He traveled for days under cover of the brush, dense from the fall rainy season. He found that Bulgaria was trying to regain control of much of the land that had been awarded to Greece after the First Balkan War. He would have to travel further west than he had anticipated if he were to find Allied troops that could help him contact and reconnect with his unit.

He made his way to the port city of Kavala across

from the island of Thasos. There he thought for sure that he would meet up with Allied forces that would help him rejoin his unit, but the village, like many he came to before it, was occupied by the Bulgarian army. To survive, Henry stole what food and water he could from the homes of unsuspecting sleeping villagers.

Henry reconsidered his strategy and changed his plans. He could not keep moving west; he would have to move south and make his way to an island. Henry sat against a cold stone building wall in a dark narrow alley and took a bite of stale bread he took from the table inside. As he chewed the dry loaf, he remembered the geography of the area from his days in school. He was in Kavala, which meant, if his memory served him correctly, the island of Thasos was almost due south of his current position. The only drawback was the considerable amount of water between the mainland and the island.

Henry considered backtracking to the port village of Keramoti, where the distance of the mainland and the island of Thasos was much shorter. He rejected this plan after realizing that the whole area was under Central Powers occupation and that the narrower straight would be more heavily monitored and protected. He decided to head for the island from his current position in the hopes that it was still under Allied control.

Henry waited until nightfall and backtracked his way to the eastern side of the city. Then he went south through trees and thick brush until he could hear the water lapping against a rocky shoreline. The smell of the ocean air and the cool breeze energized him and filled him with confidence. He knew his plan would not fail. He crept his way down a sloping hill that opened up onto a rocky shoreline. To his right, Henry saw a sandy beach. Several hundred yards along the beach, he saw a dock with a small fishing boat tied to it just aft of a larger commercial boat. Henry would take the small boat and row his way to the island.

Henry slowly and cautiously approached the dock, keeping himself on the edge of the beach and the tree line. As he got closer to the dock, he saw a Bulgarian guard standing watch on the dock. Henry slowly backed his way to the east and crawled along the sand into the water. He swam along the shoreline slowly, keeping his feet on the sand underneath when he could. He quietly made his way around the larger steam-driven fishing trawler and swam to the smaller boat. Henry took out the knife that his father had given him, cut the rope that kept the small boat tethered to the dock, and quietly pushed the boat straight back to the end of the dock. Henry waited a few seconds, listening for footsteps or any noise from the wooden planks above. All was silent. He gave the boat a slight push away from the dock and quietly climbed inside. Once he was in the boat, Henry found two oars, and to his delight, a small outboard motor lying on the keel of the small boat.

Henry rowed himself out to a safe distance and then attached the motor to the stern of the small boat. He found the spark plug wrapped in a rag, and he screwed it into place and connected the wire. Then he grasped the handle of the motors crank, and with a quick turn clockwise, the motor spun into action. Henry opened the throttle all the way with his thumb, and the three-horse motor carried him into the safety of open water. Henry thought he may have heard a couple of gunshots off in the distance from the direction he had just come, but he was confident that he had initially rowed himself out of range.

Henry silenced the motor and returned to rowing the boat as he neared the island. He needed to be cautious. If this island was also in the control of the Central Powers, he would need to escape as quickly and quietly as he had arrived. Henry found a quiet stretch of beach to the south of a peninsula. He dragged the boat as far onto the sandy beach as he could. Then he quietly made his way inland.

Henry headed east into the island's interior as the sun rose to reveal his surroundings to him. He crawled his way, alongside a narrow gravel roadway, until the road ended at a single-strip runway. Henry saw one hangar on the south end of the runway. There were two men standing guard. Henry made his way around through the bushes toward the hangar. He peered through a window and saw six aircraft inside.

Six Morane-Sauliner G aircraft sat waiting within the hangar. The planes were fabric-covered with wooden frames. The Morane-Sauliner G was a notable French aircraft that could easily reach speeds of over seventy-five miles per hour and altitudes of over two thousand meters. These particular racing monoplanes had been modified. Their wings had been re-mounted above the plane's fuselage, parasol fashion. This arrangement would allow the pilots much greater visibility. Henry noted the fin flash of the Imperial Russian Air Service. These were Allied reconnaissance aircraft.

Henry crept around the corner of the hangar and saw that the two men standing guard in the early morning light were both wearing uniforms of the Imperial Russian Air Force. Henry ducked back behind the corner of the hangar and considered how he would approach these men. He had to be careful. They may shoot him on site if they misunderstood his intentions. Henry decided he would approach slowly with his hands held high and hope for the best.

"Ne dvigaysya," Henry heard the voice behind him say just as he felt the cold steel barrel of the man's 7.63mm Mauser C96 press against the back of his skull. Henry stood and slowly raised his hands in the air.

"I'm Irish," Henry said in a soft and even tone.

"Obernis," the man said calmly, then once again with more force. "Obernis!"

The man grabbed Henry by his shoulder and spun him around. The man holding the semi-automatic pistol was dressed in a black tunic with engineer buttons. Red shoulder boards signified the man as a warrant officer. On his left breast pocket, the man wore a pilot's badge: a two-headed imperial eagle holding a crossed propeller and sword in its talons—a badge that was awarded to each pilot by the czar himself.

"English?" the man with the gun asked Henry.

"Yes, I speak English," Henry replied.

"No trespass," the man said.

Henry's attention was taken from the pistol that was still pointed at him to a small dark spot in the sky. The hum of the incoming aircraft grew louder as it drew near. Henry saw plumes of black smoke pouring out of the engine of the plane as it neared. He pointed to the approaching plane and shouted. "Incoming!"

The man with the gun turned around and watched as the plane came crashing down onto the runway. The plane hit the ground wheels first, then cart wheeled end over end as it broke apart, leaving burning pieces of frame and fabric strewn along the runway.

Henry bolted toward the cockpit of the plane. He ran as fast as his long legs would carry him. He reached into the burning compartment where the pilot lay unconscious and pulled the man out. He then dragged the man by his shoulders away from the burning wreckage toward the hangar. Seconds later, the man who had been holding Henry at gunpoint took up the pilot's legs and helped Henry carry the man into the hangar.

"Poluchit' pomoshch'!" the warrant officer shouted to one of the guards as he and Henry carried the man past them into the hangar. Henry and the Russian warrant officer laid the pilot onto a table.

"You are ally," the warrant officer said to Henry.

Henry ripped the pilot's tunic open and saw the bullet hole in the man's left shoulder that likely caused the sloppy landing.

"I need water and bandages!" Henry shouted as he pressed his hands onto the wound to stall the bleeding.

The man stared at Henry for a moment.

"Vrach," the man said as he continued to stare at

Henry. Then he translated himself, realizing Henry's language barrier. "Doctor."

"Yes, doctor," Henry said, thinking the man would call for one. "I need bandages and water, now!" he said more assertively.

"Binty, uh, bandag," the warrant officer agreed. He then ran into a room which must have been an office within the hangar to get a first aid kit.

Henry pressed hard against the man's shoulder and began to pray. He prayed that the man wouldn't die. Henry prayed that the man would live to fly another day. He prayed that the man's wounds would not cripple him for life.

The warrant officer returned with a roll of bandages. When Henry was about to remove his hands from the pilot's shoulder to take them, he noticed a warm, hard object pressing against the palm of his hand. Henry scooped at the object with his fingers and held it up so that he could see it in the light. It was a bullet. The slug that had pierced the man's shoulder had come out in Henry's hands as he prayed over the man. Henry took the bandages from the warrant officer and handed the man the bullet. He wrapped the man's shoulder and, just as he finished tucking the bandage within itself, the medical truck arrived.

Two men carrying a stretcher came into the hangar, collected the pilot, and put him into the back of the truck. The warrant officer spoke to the two men for a brief moment and then motioned to Henry for him to join the men in the truck.

"Spasibo," the man said as he shook Henry's hand.

"You're welcome," Henry replied, understanding a thank you when he heard one, regardless of the language.

Henry rode with the men to a base camp near the docks north of the peninsula. As men carried the wounded pilot into a tent, Henry was led into another.

"We cannot thank you enough for saving our comrade, Doctor...." a large man said. He paused while waiting for Henry to supply the missing component to his phrase.

"Calhoun," Henry added. "My name is Henry Calhoun."

"Ah, Doctor Calhoun!" The large Russian general said as he grabbed Henry in a quick and firm bear hug. "We are fortunate to have you here," the man continued. "Our doctor was killed, and his replacement does not arrive until tomorrow. We have several wounded men that need urgent care. Will you help my men?"

A rush of fear washed over Henry. *What if I'm not able to help anyone?* He asked himself. *What if I actually hurt someone? I need to get back to my unit.*

"Are you an ally?" the Russian general asked Henry, breaking the silence.

"Yes," Henry answered. "I actually got separated from my unit. If I could get to a radio, I could let them know I'm alive."

"Please, Doctor. My men cannot wait," the general pleaded. "Go into the tent and help my men. When you are done, we will get you to wherever you need to go."

One of the men from the medical truck led Henry by the arm to the medical tent. Three men lay on tables suffering from second and third degree burns over most of their bodies. The one man who had been shot and just brought in was lying on another. A fifth man, missing an arm, lay on another.

Henry went from man to man examining each injury, assessing the severity of each one, trying to make an order of priority as to which man needed help the most. A young Russian soldier followed Henry very closely, waiting for instruction. He was there to assist.

Henry told the young soldier to change the bandages and to apply fresh salve to each of the burn victims as he attended to the man with the missing arm. The moans from the burned men were almost as unbearable for Henry to hear as watching the flies feast on their bodies was to watch.

Henry approached the unconscious young man and un-bandaged the man's shoulder. A tourniquet that had been used to stop the bleeding was still in place, halfway between the man's shoulder and the location where his elbow would have been if he still had it. The tourniquet had been on the man's arm just below his shoulder for over a day. The skin around the tourniquet was swollen and puffy. The flesh below had turned ashen gray and dusky purple in color. The mangled remains of muscle and bone that protruded from the end were dark and dry.

Henry had no clue as what to do to help the man, but he was fairly certain that an amputation further up the man's arm was most likely what would save him from dying from sepsis.

Henry thought of the nail that was within his pocket. He hoped the nail from the table that healed him from four gunshots would be powerful enough to heal these men. *If not heal,* Henry thought to himself, *at least it might keep them from suffering.*

Henry took the nail out of his pocket and cupped it in the palm of his hand. He then took the man's shredded appendage in his hands and began to pray. Henry prayed that this young man be saved from his suffering. He prayed the young man be forgiven from any sin he may have ever committed. Henry prayed that the young man be given the chance to live and see his home and his family once again. As Henry prayed over the young soldier, he felt a hand on his shoulder. Henry looked and saw a man wearing a black robe with the white collar of a priest standing next to him. The priest joined Henry in praying over the wounded soldier.

When they finished praying, Henry noticed the man's arm was noticeably different. He could no longer see bone and muscle protruding from the end of the wound. Fresh skin had grown around the wound, and the purple-grey color was replaced by the light pink color of healthy skin. Henry re-pocketed the nail and removed the tourniquet. The priest patted Henry on the shoulder, smiled, and left the tent.

The young assistant that had been helping Henry with the burn victims left the tent as well. Henry stuck his head out of the makeshift clinic and saw that most of the men had gathered in a line heading into a large building at the end of the encampment. Henry knew a chow line when he saw one. He decided to forgo dinner and help the men within the tent while he could do so with privacy. He pulled the tables of the three burned men closer together so that he could touch them two at a time while he prayed. After a few moments of prayer, Henry noticed the men's moaning had silenced. Their breathing had settled into calm rhythms as they slept. Henry pulled back some of the bandages and saw scar tissue fully forming over places where exposed char had been. Exhausted, Henry found an empty gurney, laid himself on it, and fell asleep.

The next morning, Henry was awakened by the sound of screaming. A sailor from the Imperial Russian Navy supply ship that had just docked several yards away from the encampment had gotten his leg caught in a watertight door as the ship suddenly listed while maneuvering through an underwater mine field several days earlier. The heavy steel door slammed shut on the deckhand's leg, shattering the bone and nearly severing it completely. The sailor had been kept alive by the ship's medic, but gangrene had set in the man's leg and so they brought him to the field hospital for the amputation.

Henry stood and came toward the man as he was laid upon an operating table. The two stretcher-bearers that had brought him in, along with three other Russian sailors, were ushered out of the tent by the priest that had prayed with Henry earlier. Henry looked around the room and saw that the three burn victims, the man with the missing arm, and the gunshot pilot had all been removed from the tent.

"Where is everyone?" Henry asked.

"You have healed them, Doctor," the priest replied. "They are all having a meal in the mess hall. This man is badly injured and is in need of your attention."

The priest apprised Henry on the sailor's condition and informed him that the ship had just docked. The ship that was bringing the camp's replacement surgeon was scheduled to dock the next morning, and if Henry did not heal the man, he may not live long enough to wait.

Henry noticed the injured sailor was repeating the same phrase over and over.

"What is he saying?" Henry asked.

"He is afraid he won't dance at his wedding," the priest replied. "He won't live to have a wedding if you don't remove his leg."

Henry felt for the man. The tone of his plea reminded him of McDonough. Henry fought back tears as he asked the priest for a moment alone with the man.

"I will assist you," the priest told Henry. "You are a man who prays. I will sit at the end of the bed and pray as well as you perform your medicine."

The priest sat in a chair at the foot of the operating table, closed his eyes, and began to pray. Henry carefully pulled the nail out of his pocket and cupped it in his hand. He looked around the room to make sure that no one saw the nail. The sailor was writhing in pain, and the priest was praying. Henry placed his hands on the man's leg above the wound and began to pray. A thick mixture of blood and greenish yellow puss oozed from the wound. The stench of rotting flesh filled the air throughout the tent. The flow of blood stopped and the greenish yellow liquid that streamed out from under the man's leg turned clear like water and then stopped flowing as well. The odor from the man's wound dissipated, and so did his screams. The sailor went quiet. Henry quickly put the nail back into his pocket and pulled the hospital sheet back, revealing the man's leg. Bruising was visible, along with tears in the flesh that were beginning to heal. The bone above the man's knee appeared to no longer be broken, and there were no signs of gangrene. Henry replaced the sheet over the man and sat in a wooden chair next to the table he had earlier used as a bed.

The priest stood and went to the injured sailor. The two men spoke to each other in Russian. Henry could not follow along with the conversation, but at the end of the conversation, the sailor looked to Henry and said what he assumed was thank you. Henry smiled and nodded at the man. The priest then gestured to Henry to follow him, and the two men left the medical tent and went to another tent, where the general and two sailors awaited them. The priest and the general had a brief conversation in

Russian. Then the two men turned and addressed Henry.

"Doctor Calhoun," the general began. "You have proven yourself to be a gifted surgeon. We would like to keep you here."

A quick wave of panic wafted over Henry. "I really need to return to my unit, General." Henry protested.

"Yes, yes," the general said. "I believe you have left us with no injured soldiers. I believe we can allow you to leave before our replacement surgeon arrives. I have good news for you. We have used Allied radio to locate your unit. The supply ship that docked earlier and brought you your most recent patient will be taking you to your unit. Please, follow these two sailors to their ship. It will be leaving within the hour. I thank you for your assistance. My men thank you even more."

Henry followed the two sailors and got onto the steamer. They took him to what appeared to be a small private berthing compartment below decks. *This must be officer's quarters*, Henry thought to himself. Soon, the ship and Henry were underway.

The ship sailed from the small island in the Aegean Sea, through the Sea of Marmara, past Istanbul, and into the Black Sea. Once in the Black Sea, the steamer headed north.

By this time, Henry had suspected that the Russian

general had lied and he was not headed to where his unit was. He questioned his two Russian escorts as to their intentions, but neither man spoke a word to him during his trip. Henry was a prisoner, although he was allowed to move about the ship freely. At no point throughout the trip was Henry without the two escorts. One evening, Henry was tempted to make a run for one of the ship's lifeboats, but he changed his mind when he examined the rigging. He knew he would never get the boat into the water and away from the ship before he was captured and returned to his small stateroom.

The supply ship finally docked in Odessa, where the air had grown noticeably cold, frosting Henry's lungs with each breath. The sky was a dark grey. One of his captors draped a heavy overcoat across Henry's shoulders and led him off of the supply ship and onto the dock. Henry and the two sailors transferred to a smaller paddleboat that took them up the Dnieper River into Russia. Once on the smaller paddleboat, Henry's requests for answers became more frequent and ardent until he could no longer stand the silence. On one particular evening, as depression and rage took hold of Henry, he lashed out at one of his stoic guards, striking him in the jaw. The second sailor struck Henry immediately with a heavy cane across the temple before the other guard produced a pair of handcuffs and shackled Henry's hands together.

"You will not escape," the man told Henry with a thick Russian accent.

"But why have you kidnapped me?" Henry asked the man for what seemed the hundredth time, "Where are you taking me?"

Henry's questions still went unanswered. Henry spent several days shackled on the river boat as it snaked the Dnieper River deep into Russia. Every day became colder as ice took hold of the edges of the river. Henry found himself continually grasping the nail in his pocket out of both paranoia and comfort. Every morning, he woke from phantom-filled nightmares, fearing that the nail would be discovered and taken off his person.

Soon after the paddleboat passed Kiev, Henry noticed the river widened for a while then forked into two smaller ice-patched rivers. The paddleboat docked at Strakholissya, and once again, Henry and his two Russian escorts transferred to an even smaller boat. The small river steamer had one stack, roughly seven feet tall, and was barely large enough to fit Henry, his two escorts and the boat's pilot. The smaller boat continued up the winding Dnieper River all the way to Mogilev. Occasionally one of the men would have to stand on the bow of the steamer and, using a long pole with a pointed metal end, chip at the ice, allowing the boat to continue through it. Once in Mogilev, the small steamer docked, and Henry's close-lipped escorts transported him through a military checkpoint. He was then placed into the back of a truck and driven to the Russian Army headquarters. One of the two escorts got out of the truck and went into a building.

Henry peered through the canvas flap at the back of the truck and saw a small boy, roughly 11 years old, being carried by a man. The boy was dressed akin to a Russian general, complete with a child-sized saber dangling from a belt around his waist. The man carried the boy to the truck and let him down to stand at his side. Then, the man called to Henry's other escort, still in the truck, and lifted the canvass flap for the young boy to see Henry.

The boy looked at Henry with caring and curious eyes. He asked the man who had been carrying him a question. Henry couldn't decipher the question, not having a firm grasp on the Russian language, but the man's reply was clear.

"Da Alexei," the man replied as he lifted the boy onto his shoulder and walked back to the bench where they had been sitting.

The first escort returned from the building accompanied by two new soldiers dressed in heavy winter wear. The men marched to the back of the truck, where the second escort hopped out, leaving Henry alone.

Henry watched through the flap of the truck as the four Russian soldiers huddled together, exchanging pleasantries. After several moments, the two sailors who had been Henry's captors walked off towards another building in the distance. One of the new soldiers, a feldwebel or the equivalent of a British sergeant, approached Henry. The man smiled a yellowy grin at Henry, and in broken English said, "Welcome to Russia. British, da?"

"Irish," Henry replied.

"Same side, you and I."

"Then why am I here? Why am I a prisoner?" Henry pleaded.

"Calm yourself. No prisoner. Doctor."

Henry took several deep breaths. "Where are you taking me?"

The feldwebel smiled. "To hospital. At the palace of Prince Felix Yusupov. Cousin of Alexei." The man threw a glance over his shoulder at the young boy. The young boy was sitting high on the shoulders of the man watching over him, who pretended to nay and trot like a horse as the boy laughed. The feldwebel continued, "The prince requests your presence. Many wounded. You heal them, yes?"

"I have to get back to my regiment."

"Yes. The Irish. After you heal them," the man said, reassuring Henry with a hearty pat on the shoulder. The soldier revealed a key, lifted Henry's wrists, and unlocked his shackles. "Food, Doctor?"

As the feldwebel helped Henry down from the truck, a bone-shattering cry pierced the air. Henry's eyes instantly diverted in the direction of the scream. The feldwebel and Henry looked back in the direction where the young boy had been playing. The soldier who was carrying the young prince on his shoulders had fallen in the snow. The boy did not appear to have any external injuries from the minor fall; however, the young boy was not like other children. He was the heir to the Russian crown, and ever since he was a toddler, Alexei's parents, Tsar Nicholas II and Tsarina Alexandra, hid his illness from the world. As the boy lay in the arms of his protector, his insides began to flood with blood.

His protector yelled for assistance. He desperately needed the only man entrusted to treat Alexei's malady. "Rasputin. Idi Rasputina," the soldier cried out as he lifted the weeping boy to carry him to safety. The child's second protector bolted to find Rasputin. Without immediate care, the boy risked bleeding to death.

Henry watched as the boy was lifted and carried toward a large brick building by his companion.

"I can help him," Henry said to the feldwebel.

"Yes, Yes," the feldwebel replied as he and Henry ran to catch up with the hurt boy.

Henry and his escort ran into the building, passed two entry guards and ran down a long corridor lined with doors. They turned and entered one of the rooms on the left. The room was fashioned into the boy's bedroom. The boy was laid onto a bed, and the young prince's guard quickly stepped in front of Henry, blocking his path as he entered the room.

"Move, I can help!" Henry exclaimed.

"Het!" the Russian prince's bodyguard nervously replied. "Rasputin!"

Henry spun around and looked at the feldwebel as the cries from the boy grew louder and more agonizing.

"I can help," Henry repeated himself to his escort.

"Vrach," the feldwebel said to the boy's bodyguard as he placed his hand on the man's arm that was outstretched toward Henry's chest. "Irish vrach."

The soldier stepped aside and allowed Henry to examine the boy. Henry saw no visible signs of injury, aside from the boy's writhing. Henry felt the boy's arms, legs, and neck, checking for broken bones. He felt none.

Henry turned to the two men standing behind him and asked, "What is wrong with him?" The feldwebel turned to the other man, and the two men spoke quietly together for a few moments, although to Henry and the screaming boy it seemed like an eternity. After their brief discussion, the feldwebel turned to Henry and in a hushed voice he said, "Tsarevich Alexei has royal disease."

Henry turned back to the boy and opened the young man's shirt, revealing his chest and abdomen. Henry saw the young boy's side turn a bluish purple as it began to bulge. He reached into his pocket to retrieve the nail as he heard a voice unknown to him exclaim from down the hall, "The little one will not die. Do not allow the doctor to bother him."

Rasputin entered the boy's bedroom, his stringy black hair and hulking frame dwarfing the door behind him. He turned his pale face and hypnotic eyes onto the occupants as he took a moment to assess the situation. He saw Alexei lying on his bed with a large bruise enveloping his right side. Henry, a man Rasputin had never seen before, stood over the boy, his hands folded in prayer.

"Leave us." The mystic said to the two soldiers as he peered down upon them with deep-set green eyes.

The two soldiers quickly left the room and waited in the hall.

The towering mystic closed the door after the soldiers' retreat and turned his attention onto Henry and the boy.

By this time, Henry had placed his hands on the boy's side while continuing to pray. The boy's cries quieted, and the distention of the boy's abdomen receded, as did the discoloration. Rasputin saw the healing take place, and his wild, hypnotic eyes seemed to lose their intensity as the power of what he was witnessing overcame him, leaving him with a sense of vulnerability. Rasputin suddenly felt threatened. He was a man who, as of late, knew what it was like to be hated. His association with the Romanovs, especially Tsarina Alexandra, who viewed the mystic as a close advisor, friend and direct connection to God, had left the Russian people cause to criticize the Royal Family. The war had already claimed over one million Russian lives and left many faced with starvation. In times of great depression, choosing to blame others for one's hardship was easy to do, and the majority of the Russian people chose to place that blame on Rasputin. The bold man had never experienced a healer to be his equal, and yet here, a stranger, placed the hand of God on the young prince and removed the boy's affliction. This incident had the power to effectively remove Rasputin completely from the company of the royal family. The disreputable monk knew he had to act quickly. He was the only one, apart from the young Irish stranger, to witness the healing. Rasputin considered his options. He was a boaster and womanizer, not a murderer, but perhaps it was time for that to change.

Henry opened his eyes and placed his hand into his pant pocket, safely depositing the nail in it. He looked down upon the sleeping boy and saw that once again, God had allowed him the power to heal. Henry smiled as he noticed a shadow envelop his entire body. Just as Henry began to turn, a giant fist came crashing down upon his head and all went dark.

Minutes later, the finely groomed, bearded face of Tsar Nicholas II was cloaked in worry as he swiftly moved down the hallway towards his son's bedroom. The feldwebel and the young boy's two protectors followed suit. Nicholas quickly swung open the door and entered to find Alexei sitting up, laughing as the mystic Rasputin playfully pinched the boy's nose. Nicholas' heart filled with relief.

"Papa," Alexei said as he stretched his arms out to his father, who delicately embraced the boy.

Rasputin watched the loving father kiss the boy on the forehead. Then Nicholas peered over at Rasputin and nodded in thanks. Rasputin humbly bowed his head and rose to his feet. The three soldiers glanced at one another, perplexed by the sudden disappearance of Henry.

Henry slowly opened his eyes to the familiar sounds of a steamer engine pumping away. He immediately shoved his hand into his pocket to feel for the cold iron of the nail. His travel companion was safe and sound.

The mad monk had given Henry quite the clobbering before having one of his faithful followers smuggle Henry out of Russia and onto a steamer headed for Stockholm. Meanwhile, Rasputin took full credit for the healing of Alexei, gloating to the Tsarina about how he saw the image of the Virgin Mary reach her blessed hand down upon his as he healed the tsarina's son. This fabrication placed Rasputin once again firmly under the protection of the tsar and above reproach from his enemies within the Russian government.

Henry disembarked the steamer in Stockholm and began the long trek across Sweden and Norway, taking up odd jobs to help fund his way back home. He managed to reach the shipyards of Skudenshavn, Norway, where he took up work until he'd earned his passage to Aberdeen, Scotland.

In spring 1916, for the first time in what felt like

years, Henry felt the weight of world lift off his shoulders as the ship he was aboard neared the coast of Scotland. The lush green hills behind the tan beach of Aberdeen may not have been his homeland but ran a wonderful second as he walked off the ship and onto solid ground. Henry fell to his knees, smelled the crisp clean fragrance of the grass, and thanked God he was alive. The smell of sulfur, sage, and rotten, bloated flesh was cleansed from his senses, and the dew from the grass moistened his lips. With one hand, he held the nail, and with the other, he held his mother's locket and breathed a long, glorious breath. After taking some time to simply meditate on his ordeal, he stood up and turned his attention to two pressing items: one, contacting his parents in Dublin, and two, finding a way back to his regiment.

There was a tiny telegraph office located near the shipyard. Henry compiled a telegraph and had the telegraph operator, an older gentleman, send the message off to the post office in Dublin, where his mother worked as a telegraph operator. Henry walked outside, found a comfortable bench that overlooked the North Sea, and sat down to wait for a reply. A few hours passed as he anxiously waited. He had hoped for a quicker reply, but perhaps his mother was not at work today. Then suddenly, Henry felt a tap on his shoulder.

"For you, mate," the older gentleman said, handing Henry the reply telegraph.

"Thank you," Henry said as he zealously opened the message. Henry's eyes darted back and forth as he read the message from his mother.

Words cannot express how overjoyed I am, my son, to learn that you are alive. We received a telegraph from the army last August informing us that you had died a decorated hero in battle. Your father was very proud of you and stricken with grief upon hearing the news.

His mood suddenly turned from joy to sorrow as he read on.

It pains me to tell you that your father was killed this past April 26th during a terrible week-long riot. I have taken lodging with my sister. Please come home soon. I miss you dearly.

Six months later, Henry stood near the Fountain of the Sacrament in the walled enclave of Vatican City. There he was met by a middle-aged Cardinal, with whom Henry relayed his fantastic tale of Father Keshishian and the chapel underground laden with holy treasures. He pleaded hard to convince the cardinal to aid in a search to rescue Father Keshishian and any survivors of the underground city. The cardinal sympathized with Henry and the plight of the Armenian priest. Unfortunately, they lived in grave times, and the cardinal was skeptical of Henry. He extended his hand towards Henry and informed him that the only form of help the Holy See was able to provide was that of prayer.

Henry squeezed the nail in his pant pocket tightly and considered whether he would be able to give it up. This relic was the only object Henry had to support his tale. *If the dangers of war were too great to risk sending a search party for the refugees, perhaps the cardinal would find the retrieval of the true cross worth the risk,* Henry thought as he rolled the nail between his fingers and palm. Henry then slowly removed the nail from his pocket, stretched his hand out to the cardinal's, and unveiled the iron relic.

"Along with my life, I have this to offer as proof," Henry said with conviction. Henry continued to passionately testify to the cardinal of the healings he had witnessed. "I do not fully understand God's plan for me, but this holy relic has brought me here. And God deserves the sole credit for its miracles. Father Keshishian understood this and was willing to risk his life to protect it. This holy relic belongs here, along with God's other treasures, that are hidden away deep under that mountain. If the Holy See will not help me, then I will go alone. I owe Father Keshishian that much." Henry dropped the nail into the cardinal's palm.

The cardinal peered deeply into Henry's eyes. There was truth there. Without a doubt. There was truth. "Please wait here, Doctor Calhoun." The cardinal left Henry in the gardens and walked into a nearby building.

Henry slowly walked toward the bubbling water of the monumental fountain. He raised his left hand to his heart and rubbed his chest bone. The oval bump from his mother's locket that still hung about his neck pressed into his skin. The sensation caused Henry to take the locket into his hand and remove the necklace from around his neck. He continued to massage his chest; a pain he couldn't quite explain throbbed where the locket had momentarily embedded in his flesh.

Henry looked down at the locket and was able to see his reflection peer back at him from the crystal fountain waters in the lower basin. As he stared at himself, he thought fondly of his parents, Matthew and Catherine, until a hint of sadness overcame him. Tears gently began to collect behind the damns of his eyelids. He opened the locket to gaze upon their faces.

The clasp clicked open, and resting on top of the picture of his father was the broken tip from the holy nail he had handed over to the Vatican. Henry blinked to clear his eyes, causing a teardrop to fall into the locket, wetting the nail tip. The deep blackish grey color of the iron shifted to a dark crimson. Henry lifted the locket closer to his eyes to examine it. *Is it possible?* Henry thought to himself. The tip appeared grafted with blood.

"Doctor," a voice said in a heavy Italian accent, startling Henry.

Henry closed the locket and placed the necklace back around his neck. "Yes," he said as he turned around.

The owner of the voice was Father Michelli, the man tasked with maintaining the museums along with all of the treasures of the Holy See. Was the man here to further interrogate Henry about the nail? Or was the Vatican willing to aid in his quest to search for Father Keshishian and the people and holy relics under his protection?

"The Vatican would like to discuss a job opportunity with you, Doctor Calhoun," the priest said. "Would you consider following me?"

Henry nodded and followed the priest. The two men walked off, deep into the gardens of Vatican City and towards a private set of secure buildings. It is here where Henry would begin his new life and unlock knowledge beyond his wildest dreams.

Thank you for journeying with The Iron Relic. We'd love to read your feedback. Please rate or leave a review for this book on such sites as Amazon and Goodreads under the book page for: *The Iron Relic: Origins*. connect with us on Twitter: @TheIronRelic, Facebook: The Iron Relic Book Series or on the world wide web at www.theironrelicbook.com

Please continue the saga by reading the other books in the series:

The Iron Relic Book I: The Crossing, Henry Calhoun, now 119 years old and on his deathbed, passes the relic and its secrets down to his great grandson Adam Calhoun, a young oncologist who doesn't believe in the power behind the relic until one of his patients is miraculously healed. The legacy soon becomes a nightmare bequest as mystery, murder and miracles ensue, with shadowy figures and thugs for hire crossing paths with Vatican emissaries and forbidden archaeological excavations. As his family implodes, Doctor Adam Calhoun, fights not only for his life, but that of those he loves.

The Iron Relic Book II: Revelations (Due to be released in 2016), the thrilling, heart wrenching conclusion to the Calhoun Family saga in which Adam digs deep into his family origins. Enemies and allies are revealed, hidden history is uncovered, government agencies collide and the true power of the pendant, and the iron relic it protects, portends a second coming.

ABOUT THE AUTHORS

James Stevenson

James Stevenson was born and raised in Hannibal, Missouri. He was catholic schooled from the first through the seventh grades. James joined the U.S. Navy in 1988 and served until 1992. He now resides in Los Angeles, California where he works as an actor under the stage name Dallas James.

Bobby Hundley

Bobby Hundley has always had a fascination with history, archeology and medicine which made *The Iron Relic Book Series* a true passion piece for him. As a child, he grew up hearing stories of miraculous healings from his own Papa, who was a strong man of faith. He now resides in Los Angeles, California where he works as a producer, writer and actor. He has a children's book series: *The Adventures of Princess Lainey* coming out in 2016.

To learn more about The Iron Relic Book Series, please visit us on the World Wide Web at

www.theironrelicbook.com

www.ingramcontent.com/pod-product-compliance
Lightning Source LLC
Chambersburg PA
CBHW071313130626
46556CB00004B/1591